# THE
# SALMAGUNDI

## AN ANTHOLOGY

67 Press
**Winston Salem, North Carolina**

ISBN: 978-0692228258

We dedicate this book to our families and friends.

To Caroline and Ali, thank you for the gift of unconditional support and love. Know that your bizarre husbands love you dearly.

To our contributing writers, let's do it again sometime...

# TABLE OF CONTENTS

# LOVE, INFIDELITY, DRUGS, DEATH AND DINOSAURS...AN INTRODUCTION

The stories that follow are the product of a small sample of the immense talent banging away on keyboards, scribbling in notebooks and working on their craft. They do this because they love it, because they find meaning in it. After all, why else would they decide to become writers? This is a gig that pays big for only a few; the rest of us have to put our heads down, keep our butts in the seat and write–because it's what we are driven to do.

We're fortunate at 67 Press. We get to read the inspirations and tribulations of a new generation of writers. It's the reason we started this business and it's the reason you're holding this book right now, because you love good stories, too.

As we worked our way through all the submissions and began to whittle the list down to the final pieces, we went in with no particular theme in mind. Yet these seemingly disparate tales work together to present a larger vision of humanity, albeit on the small scale.

This is the beauty of the short story. In limiting the number of words we use, we're forced to make them count. The author is constantly working to distill the world into easily managed bits, without stripping them of their complexities. Short stories, more than any other brand of fiction, show us the significance of the smallest actions or thoughts. Through their minimalism, they should show us a glimpse of something bigger.

We think the twenty stories that make up "The Salmagundi" are everything short stories should be. They tell us what it's like to be human and they do it through some pretty universal themes – love, infidelity, drugs, death and even, dinosaurs.

It's going to be a hell of a ride folks, hope you enjoy it as much as we do...

67 Press

# THE SALMAGUNDI

# SITTING UNDER THE PIER

## EMILY AUMAN

I always sit under the pier. Those overly-commercialized beaches, with resorts lining the shore so you can't actually see the entire beach, are filled with people just dying to stand on the pier. In fact, these consumers are so excited about standing on the pier they actually pay money to stand on the pier. I sit under the pier. I guess that makes me different, not special, just different. I didn't always come to these beaches. When I was young we went to beaches that were quiet and only had a few restaurants and the air always smelled like salt instead of suntan lotion and the ocean was clear enough to see my feet instead of too crowded to check. That was before my family fell apart, now we stay at the popular beaches because, surprisingly enough, they are less expensive. Entropy; things fall apart, I learned that in my freshman biology class at community college. I'm starting to learn that while biologically, entropy is a commonplace theme, it is mentally, too. At this one beach, there's a Ferris wheel that spins and spins even if there's no one on it. It's always scared me, so I stop looking at it and sit under the pier.

No one else is ever under the pier, which is strange to me because it's more fascinating than anywhere else on the beach. Of course, maybe it's more fascinating because there's no one under it to ruin it. I think people like being on top of the pier because they like looking down and feeling superior to the things that would normally scare them, like the sharks in the water or the people they don't understand, the people who sit under the pier. I remember one time when I was a child, before my family entropy, when my dad took me onto the pier and I was on top of it. I looked down and thought how much bigger the ocean looked but how much bigger I felt, and I felt greater than everything else. I think people like that feeling, I don't.

All my favorite books are about unhappy rich people. I think it's because unhappy rich people are always learning the things I already know, like how the wheel keeps spinning even when there isn't anyone on it and how sitting below the pier is more beautiful than being on top of it. I already know all this and I can laugh at the mistakes the characters make because I know better, and I guess that's my version of standing on the pier, looking down at what frightens me.

# THE JOKE

## BARCLAY JONES

I stood in the doorway, watching her lay diagonal across the bed. She was falling back into heavy sleep. She'd been laughing just a few minutes before. I like her laugh, I like that it still happened. I like when I'm the one inspiring it. I stayed a minute longer, listening to her breathe. Then I walked out as usual.

I drive the same way every day. It's one of only three ways I can drive my son to school. It's the same way I used to drive to work; when I worked. I used to work a lot. It slowly ate my soul but I pretended it didn't. It was harder to play the game after the breakdown. Those days I barely got out of bed. I fell asleep at my desk and sometimes in the bathroom.

The drive to school reminds me of back then, but only in passing. Mostly I just drive.

There's a Gas-Mart on the way. I spent a lot of time at the Gas-Mart back in the day. My "unwind on the way home" beer. Something cold and tall, preferably malt liquor, something strong, like me after a long day. I still want a beer whenever I see the old 'Mart.

Billy, an old black man missing the last digit of his index finger, worked the counter. It's weird, my dad was missing the same digit; he lost it digging a well. I liked Billy; he smoked behind the counter and smelled like motor oil. We exchanged knowing glances and manly interludes. I was the white kid buying a tall beer; I liked to think he could identify with me.

I'll never tell a soul, but I think that was it. I think it was those beers that tipped me over the edge. I come from a long line of men who drank, they did it every day. I never thought a thing about it. Her parents drank; she never even considered it. Drinking was what we did. But still, I think that was the start.

I bought a pack of cigarettes from Billy on my way home one day and started smoking. I'd never been a smoker, but suddenly I couldn't get enough. Every time I lit one up it was like I was fighting the devil, taming his magic, inhaling his strength to calm the madness. It didn't feel weird or out of the ordinary, it was just another part of my day. I remember having a drink with a friend after work and she expressed her concern. I was flummoxed; I couldn't understand why she thought there was a problem. "It's never good when someone who's never smoked suddenly starts smoking. It's a sign of instability." I stopped getting beers with her after work.

I guess my smoking coincided with my first panic attack. I don't remember exactly when they started, but they became so frequent I learned to live with them. I thought they were normal, like my smoking.

I talked to myself in gas station bathroom mirrors; I didn't know who I was talking to. I banged my head against walls and I drove as fast as I could. I drove around drinking and talking to myself. Soon I stopped talking to myself, unhappy with what I was saying. I kept driving though, and I kept drinking. I guess that's when I really started drinking alone.

Eventually I did some things. Things I may not be able to come back from. But I did them all the same.

There's some distance between us and the things that happened, but time hasn't closed the distance between us. When I think about it, I don't know if I'll ever cross it. But when I don't, when

I let myself fall into the patter of the day, sometimes, it doesn't seem so far.

Today's one of those days, one of those days when she laughs. She said she fell in love with me because I made her laugh. Later on, she told me I wasn't serious enough, all I ever did was make jokes, stupid ones at that. So now, when she laughs, it's like light on my dark soul. I feel like anything is possible. If only for that moment, I can pretend that everything will be alright.

I don't work these days, so after I drop him off, I go home. She's working today, but gets to go in late, so she's still in bed when I get back. I walk into the room and hear her crying. She's under the covers, head and all, quietly crying, like she doesn't want to impose. I ask her what's wrong, but I know it's me. It's always me. I sit down beside her and think of all the times she wanted me to reach out to her and I didn't. Of all the times she wished that I would touch her and comfort her. I remember sitting, stymied, not knowing what to say and always thinking that whatever I could say would be wrong.

How can I comfort her when I'm the one she needs comfort from?

I reach out, with my big clumsy hands, and pat her on the shoulder. I pull the comforter down and softly stroke her hair, before leaning forward, kissing her cheek and gently whispering in her ear, "An old man's sitting at the bar. He's been drinking all day long. He calls the bartender over for another drink but before he can ask, he pukes all over himself. He starts to wail, 'Oh no, I'm going to be in so much trouble. My wife... my wife is going to kill me. She's going to kill me.' The Bartender, feeling sorry for him, pulls a ten out of his wallet and sticks it in the old man's puke covered shirt pocket. 'No problem fella, you go home and tell your wife somebody ELSE puked on you, and this ten bucks is what he gave you to cover the cleaning costs.' So the old man goes home and stumbles inside to his wife's disapproving gaze. She asks him why he's covered in puke, and he reaches into his pocket, pulls out the money, and gives it to her. He repeats the bartender's story, and to his amazement, finds his wife to believe him. She tells him to go change. As he walks by, she looks at the money and asks 'Hey, I thought you said he gave you a ten? This is twenty dollars.' He keeps walking and replies 'Oh yeah, I forgot to tell you, he shit in my pants, too'."

I feel her laugh between her quiet little sobs.

# CAT'S EYES

## CLODAGH O'BRIEN

All I can see are cat's eyes. A line of them glistening under a coal laced sky. I left the street lamps behind miles ago. Now it's just me, the stars, the pit of a night and those glaring eyes.

As a kid I always pushed in-between the front seats when we drove anywhere. I'd slip my knees into the gap and clamp them tight against the seats, then hook my fingers around the headrests, the filling so ancient it turned to putty in my grip. From there I had the perfect view of everything, front, back and up ahead. The only weakness was behind, and back then anything I couldn't see wasn't worth worrying about anyway.

It was a habit that used to drive my mother mad.

"It's dangerous Ollie. Especially the way your father drives."

She'd always say it, look at my father and give him a grin, one that I'd never seen her use with anyone else. He'd always grimace back, in a weird half-smile that looked like he was having a stroke. Smiling was never his forte, but at least he tried.

"At least pull the seatbelt around you Ollie. I don't want to see your head flying through the window."

To keep her happy I'd pull the belt across my stomach and lean back an inch. It wasn't any safer, but it seemed to stop the nagging.

Carolyn always complained about my driving. Told me I was impulsive and irresponsible behind a wheel. It turned out to be every wheel; bicycles, motorbikes, bumper cars, simulated car games, the lot. To me there's no point in having something that can go fast and not letting it. If it's not meant to go at that speed, then don't make it that way.

"That's a stupid argument," Carolyn would say.

"It makes perfect sense to me."

Whenever I disagreed with her the silence got edges.

Finally she'd break it with a long sigh, the tail of which sounded out—"Of course it does" and spend the rest of the time looking out the window.

Outside the wind is howling. Every now and then it makes the car shudder. I can hear its murderous whispers.

I've never been one for music in the car. All it does is fill the space with noise. My father used to drive with the music blaring. Before my mother died it was Elvis, The Beatles and Buddy Holly; anything that made your muscles twitch. She used to hum along and tap her feet lightly against the plastic mat on the floor. Afterwards it was Jeff Buckley and Nick Drake in rotation. Afterwards we only listened to tragedies.

The clock on the dashboard says it's eight, but it feels much later than that. I find winter is too fond of sleep. A season stuck in one long yawn that keeps you down for as long as it can. Out here with the city far behind is its favourite place, in a cauldron of shades and shadows.

Carolyn was meant to be with me now. She's the whole reason I'm driving in the dark.

"I can't just get up and leave work early Oliver."

From her lips, my name curdled on its way out.

"Not even for this?"

"Not for anything."

"That'll mean we're late."

Another voice sounded in the background and she muffled the phone with her hand.

"I have to go."

"I said—you know that'll mean we're late?"

"Surely an hour or two won't matter."

"It does to me."

Her exasperation made the phone hot against my ear.

"It'll be fine. I mean it's not like he's going anywhere."

I listened to the beep long after she had gone.

At work they gave me flowers. I can smell them in the back of the car, a tower of white lilies. I don't think I've ever got flowers in my life. Given them yes, but not received them and especially not from a handful of lads.

"Hey Ollie we got ya these. Ya know for him and all."

For something so delicate they weighed a lot.

Behind my eyes started to prickle, a tug at the back of my sockets.

"Thanks lads. I appreciate it."

I swallowed hard and took their shoulder slaps. One by one sorry got leached from them and I watched as they walked away, lighter.

"Look I just can't go. Something's come up and it has to be done tonight."

In front of Carolyn's office the engine churned.

"Just tell them why and it'll be fine."

"No it won't. This work doesn't just stop for things."

I turned the key making the engine hum.

"You do understand that you're not saving lives here or solving the mysteries of the universe Carolyn. It's fucking insurance."

Her breath went in fast and quick as if pulled through a straw.

"I can't talk to you when you're like this."

"Like what? Like I want to have my girlfriend beside me at my father's funeral."

"You're twisting things."

"How? How am I twisting things?"

Her eyes went steely.

"Is it not right that you should be there with me?"

"I have to get back inside."

Anger pounded my head with its fists.

"Enough of this, I'm going in there to sort this out."

Carolyn leaned down and held the door shut.

"No you won't."

"I fucking will. Enough of this bullshit."

"Just leave it Oliver. You can go on your own."

There it was, out there and in the open. Those three little words I'd tried so hard to push away... on... your...own.

"So that's it, is it? You're choosing this place."

"It's not much of a choice."

She knelt down, her fingers curled over the open window frame.

"This hasn't been right for a while."

For the first time in years there was a softness to her voice.

"You'll be alright Oliver, maybe it's better if you…"

I didn't let her finish. The spit came out with force. A perfect frothy mound that landed on her forehead and dribbled down like lava. She pulled back in shock. I turned the key and revved. In the mirror I saw her, a sprawl on the tarmac, the skirt around her hips. Someone ran out of the building towards her.


On… your… own… circles in my brain.

ON YOUR OWN.

on your own.

It's running round my grey matter of a race track trying to find the finish line. There's no escaping the words. I'm an orphan now.

Growing up we always had loads of cats. My mother used to feed any stray that came to the door with a weird mix of chicken liver and ox's tongue that they all went mad for, in the same way as catnip. It meant she was always covered in scratches.

I think she needed the affection as my father and I disliked being touched, always have done. When I was six she told me that I announced that I no longer wanted to be hugged. Apparently I said they made me itchy.

"But they're a way for people to show how much they love you."

"But I know you love me."

"Yes Ollie, but hugs are a way to show that. They're a reminder to each other."

"Well I don't need remembering. You tell me all the time."

I don't have a memory of it, so can only rely on hers.

What I wouldn't give for one of them now.

Up ahead are lights, glowing balls in the blackness. I turn the steering wheel and the tyres chatter as they move over the cat's eyes. The murderous whispers are back.

"Ollie I've told you a thousand times, lean back and put that seatbelt on."

I was defiant that day. Earlier that morning she'd given out to me for chucking one of the cats outside.

"But it bit me."

I held up my arm to show her the bloody prongs.

"I don't care. You don't treat animals that way."

So instead of pulling the seatbelt around me I ignored her.

"Ollie, do as you are told."

I carried on as if she didn't have a voice.

"Right."

She unbuckled herself and forced me back into the seat.

"Now stay right there."

As she moved back the world turned upside down.

When we finally stopped, the car was on its side. Music blared from one dangling speaker.

The bowls of lights flash, beacons in the night looking to save me. I press down hard on the accelerator. The wind throws me forward.

In the dazzle I see my father. He's in the front seat of the car in the garage, the carcass he refused to put to scrap and instead restored.

"We don't think he suffered Ollie. It's been hard for him. Even after all these years."

I can see him now, his head next to the crack in the window where he fed through the pipe.

"I guess it all finally got too much.

The smoke gushing out long after he was gone.

A beep booms through the wind. The engine roars and grumbles.

In the rumble I hear Carolyn. On our first date when we were both fifteen with no idea how life was going to turn out.

I bet I can beat you!"

"Not a hope Carolyn."

"What about a bet then? The loser buys…"

She looked around the fairground in jerks.

"One of those burgers, the Triple Fantastic."

"It's your money!"

On the count of three we ran towards the bumper cars.

"That's one," I said before racing off.

I won six to one and relished every bite of that burger.

"C'mon admit it then."

"That wasn't part of the deal."

"Well it should've been."

I thumbed a lob of tomato sauce from her chin.

"Fine! You're the bumper car king."

I stood up and jumped around. She rolled her eyes. That day I felt like I'd really won something.

Beneath my foot the accelerator thumps. The cat's eyes no longer matter. I close my eyes and wait for familiar sounds. Crash, smash, bang, whack, crack...

"I'm sorry I didn't wear a seatbelt mum."

# LET'S GO TIGERS!

## DONALD GEORGE LOSEY

It was raining on account of hurricane Irene, but this was in Philadelphia. Philly never got hurricanes until this one came along as far as I know and everyone freaked out and started stocking up for y2k all over again, but I'm from the south east and used to hurricanes doing not much at all and also am a bit on the dangerously apathetic side so me and my benzo'd 24/7, alcoholic, sort of roommate Jenna weren't worried except that maybe we wouldn't be able to get beer so we stocked up on a case of make weight and rented a couple of bad horror movies from the 70's.

It became clear very quickly that nothing worse than a moderately high amount of rain would come from Irene so we got drunk and started playing poker with pennies from a plastic coin jar as chips and listened to music and every couple of minutes we'd stop and laugh at the movie.

We both got more drunk than usual. She was low on Xanax so she drank a lot. I hadn't had any heroin for almost a month and even though at that point despite having switched from snorting to shooting wasn't addicted I was going stir crazy from being too sober all the time. So I drank a lot as well.

It's impossible to be bored on heroin. Michael Alig said that. I saw him say it on YouTube doing an interview. He used to do lots of drugs and made a lot of nightclubs in New York very (in) famous, but he also killed someone.

The Devil's Nightmare ended and we put on Long Weekend which is about an Australian couple who don't get along very well who go out into the wilderness and litter and argue and kill defenseless animals for no reason and like in all 70's exploitation horror movies where one couple who don't get along very well are the main or only characters the woman had an abortion so all the animals gang up on them and chase them around and eat them in the end. I was sad because there weren't any crocodiles. Jenna and I were both sad because we'd already seen it twice before and it was only funny with pot but the hippie / raver couple who we bought pot from had broken up earlier that month and it was too awkward to go to them for more after that. We were both certain that whoever we went to for pot would take our choosing them as a sign of siding with them or maybe even try to convince us of how horrible the other one was. They were too stupid to care about or get involved with so we just stopped smoking pot for a while. As a result Long Weekend was boring even with music and beer and poker.

I went outside for a cigarette. I didn't really want one all that badly, mostly I wanted to play in the rain. No one was outside which was very unusual since it was center city which always has at least one person wandering around all the time. So I took off my shoes and walked around the block while smoking. Still no one. I unzipped my pants and pulled my penis out which I thought was kind of funny at first and also really cool because I never thought I'd get the chance to walk around Philadelphia with my genitals outside of my pants but it felt hollow and ultimately boring somehow so I also pulled out my testicles and felt a little better.

I decided to convince Jenna to go for a walk with me since she was depressed that week and it would cheer her up even though she didn't know it would at the time. Normally she doesn't do things like that but really the whole reason she started hanging out with me was because I can be very impulsive so eventually I convinced her to go to Rittenhouse Square with me. We left our shoes under her bed.

At first no one was there and I swam in the fountain and convinced her to do it also. I'd always wanted to swim in it but normally there would have been too many people around. It felt good.

A bunch of gay guys from the Midwest showed up from one of the hotels nearby. They all pretty much looked alike. A few of them flirted with me which was nice but despite the fact that to me they all looked like clones I could tell the ones flirting with me were considered to be the least attractive of the group. Jenna loved them. There were about seven of them. She liked that they were very flamboyant and catty and if she'd asked they could've given her fashion advice which I can't do because I'm the 'bad type of gay' because I'm useless to straight girls unless they want someone to drink with and not squeeze their boobs.

One of the Ohiomos suggested we skinny dip in the fountain and we did which was nice. Jenna said she didn't look at their penises because it would have been rude and that was stupid I thought since I wanted her to tell me how she thought I compared and since it was their idea in the first place that we all get naked they wouldn't have cared.

After about five minutes or half an hour the police showed up. All the guys from the hotel got dressed very quickly and ran off but since me and Jenna weren't on ecstasy or anything and just drunk it took us a long time. Her shirt was tight and with it being wet she had a very hard time getting it back on, so we just pretended to be crocodiles and hid from the police with just our mouths and eyes above the water. Fuck the police.

After that we started to leave but other people showed up and were too drunk or friendly to notice how awkward me and Jenna were and they played in the fountain with us and invited us back to their hotel. On the way a guy who was maybe French or British flirted with Jenna and let her use his flip flops. I didn't know what to say to anyone so I just talked very loudly to no one in particular about starting a riot like in the U.K. and then one girl said that would be fun. I got excited for a minute but then realized she wasn't really serious. I stopped talking and instead stared at a hot Turkish or Iranian or something guy and wondered how all these people knew each other. Their hotel was very nice and they all seemed to mostly live on the same floor in extended stay suites.

We all took shots which I usually can't stomach unless I'm already drunk. Luckily I was a little and there was the added pressure of not wanting to throw up all over people I didn't really know.

I took about four shots.

Then an Asian chick who I hadn't noticed until that point said we should all dance and an Indian guy who was roommates with the Middle Eastern guy started looking for his iPod. Me and Jenna got very nervous because we never dance or go to parties or clubs but it didn't matter since when the music started all they did was jump around in time to the beat which was actually kind of fun even though I didn't know what to do with my hands. The song was a remix of 'Paper Planes' with just the line "No one on the corner got swagga like us. swagga swagga like us. swagga swagga like us" repeated for about five minutes which was stupid. The singer was 'M.I.A.' who apparently hates football or America or something and is from Tamil I think.

It's too bad the Tamil Tigers didn't suicide bomb her house because then we could have listened to "We Like Pizza" by "The Pizza Kids" which is also stupid but listened to the right way can sound like an unintentional cautionary tale against mindless consumerism and or the dangers of excess. Also it's catchier than the M.I.A. song.

Let's go Tigers!

Later we went to the fountain again. On the way out the black night guard man looked at us like we were crazy and I wanted to go over to his desk and tell him I wasn't a rich kid like the rest of the people I was with but that seemed too pretentious and I felt embarrassed for myself.

When we got back to the hotel the second time the Middle Eastern guy said he had pot. Me and Jenna and him and this really nice kind of nerdy brown haired girl all went to the roof to smoke and started talking about gays and it was obvious that the Middle Eastern guy was a homophobe so I decided to fuck with him. He said there was no such thing as bisexual and if a guy fucked another guy he was gay and that there was a very straight and clear line between straight and gay with no inbetween so I locked eyes with him and said that straight lines don't ever occur in nature. He asked if I was a fag and I said sort of since I'm always putting my penis in guys' mouths and butts but I never act like a fag. He was acting like a fag I said on account of how uptight he was getting. The brown haired girl tried to take my side because she thought I was being treated poorly and then changed the subject to the war which everyone agreed was stupid. She started acting like a complete faggot because her boyfriend was in the marines and she was worried because she hadn't heard from him in a while.

After that we went inside where everyone was watching Silent Hill. Jenna got very paranoid and made me paranoid by association. The only other white guy who was maybe French or British offered to let Jenna hang her clothes in his shower and borrow a towel to dry off with which I thought would make her less uncomfortable but it didn't because once she'd wrapped herself up in the towel and we'd gone back to watching the movie she kept saying things like "did they mean me?" and "can they hear me?" and "am I breathing really loud?" so I said "let's leave."

I asked the guy who had given Jenna the towel where the bathroom was even though I remembered where it was, I couldn't think of any other way to announce that we were leaving without seeming stranger than I already possibly seemed.

He said "sure" and led us to the bathroom which was only one room over and visible from where we had been sitting. I could tell that he could tell that Jenna was feeling very uncomfortable and awkward. He tried to be friendly and make jokes but Jenna thought he was making fun of her and said "go away!" in a very mean sounding quiet sort of yell and he did. We found her shorts but had trouble getting them to stay up so I gave her my belt and we left without saying goodbye. I could have since I was feeling reckless and not at all awkward at that point but I didn't feel like it so we walked from the bathroom to the hallway door without saying anything. Before the door finished closing all the way I heard someone say "bye?"

The sun was rising by the time we got outside. Jenna's feet were hurting her from having been wet all night then slapped around on asphalt. Mine were okay because I'm from the south and walk around barefoot like a hick all the time. She could barely walk because of how much drunker than me she had gotten and had to lean on me for support and kept saying she couldn't go any further and people were staring at us because it was broad daylight and the rain had stopped hours ago and we were soaking wet and stumbling with bloodshot eyes. I kept chanting little affirmations to her, barely able to keep myself standing, "Just another block and we'll stop for a cigarette and you can rest," I said. "Okay. Okay." she said. When we got to the next block I'd say, "No. Let's keep going, we can make it another block. We've come so far" and she'd get annoyed with me and say that I told her we could stop and I'd just say "so close, so close" over and over again trying to ignore all the people on stoops and in cars staring at us.

"I can't believe I let you convince me to go out. I acted like an idiot at the hotel. They were all making fun of us." "No you didn't. They liked us. They thought you were really funny and cool."

"Everyone's staring, we look ridiculous."

"No they aren't you're just being paranoid. You know you're paranoid, so you have to trust me not you. You know that."

"Okay."

The next afternoon when we both woke up we realized we had accidentally stolen someone's shorts. It was probably the white maybe French maybe British guy or the Middle Easterner. Either way it was funny.

Sometimes I wonder if the brown haired girl ever heard from her boyfriend.

# The Incident

## Michael Cooper

Bella is sick at school again and I have to get there before one or the nurse will do her bitch best to report me to CPS again. Sometimes it feels like these women don't get that I have to work two jobs to take care of her fulltime. Malcom tries, but it's not like he owes us anything.

In the review mirror I see a black Full-E BMW slide around the edge of my car to pass, *slick-dick electric car and fast.* I let him go. Look back. My mocha crow's feet walk worry down to my smeary lipstick. I'm snarling again. Fuck I'm a wreck. I grab sunglasses. No. Maybe that is the wrong way to go. Nurse Ratched might have her suspicions if I act like I'm covering something up.

I walk in the school's office. Bella is kicking her legs in a too-tall-for-a-kid chair. I scan the waiting room, tagging 3 entrances and Bella's socks are mismatched. The walls are plastered in those funky turkey hand outlines still up two weeks after Thanksgiving. The construction paper feet, beaks and wings are cut outside the lines and pasted in a slipshod way. More like they were making fun of blown-up turkeys. And the handwriting is in crayon; atrocious. No-Go at this station. She's still kicking her damn legs.

Bella has my hair and eyes. Long blue black braids. Loopy noblink infantry eyes. I had to earn mine riding in Humvees and learning from muzzle flashes. Lucky Bella, she got hers from me for free. My ancient 2012 Chevy Tahoe rumbles outside. Shit, I can hear my *Welcome Home Patriot!* license frame rattling even here inside the office with the doors closed. Need to screw it down tighter. Preventative maintenance.

I sign her out. Ratched nowhere in sight. Good. Out. I smile at the office lady in her red pinstriped smock. Sheri I think. She grimaces and says hi Jen. This is that smile you get when shit will go down later that they will disavow knowing of now. You get to know this feeling when people talk a lot behind your back but value their own imminent physical safety. My daughter looks at me. Stares through me really. I'm fucking up. I know it. They all know it. I kiss her forehead and gently put on her cover before we go out-doors. It is her favorite Miami Dolphins ball-cap given to her by her natural dad, back when dolphins seemed cute and were friendly to humans. Too damned bad they can't sort us from the infected. Guess Flipper isn't really all that smart after all. We leave.

When we get close to the Tahoe, I get a funny feeling, so I drop down prone and check the undercarriage for IEDs. Every once in a while this earns a strange look from the other parents, but I don't care. Bella's going to grow up safe. But the car ride is silent. No explosions. Bella falls asleep. We don't need to talk. Bella and I are like that.

I knew what I needed to know by the nurse's tone of voice on the phone. There was no fever she'd said, and now I'm missing work because Bella can't handle the other kids appropriately. She's been acting out lately, and the administratum are being extra careful because of the two conversion-expulsions of her class mates. They send kids home for a slight temperature, like this is an epidemic. Like we don't have things locked in tight: God Bless America.

Bella's newest outburst has earned her an incident report filed by the Vice-Principal and countersigned by Tommy's parents. A scratch fight. That little asshole probably deserved what he got. Incidents. They are always on our minds. But we don't talk. We just install break-proof glass and look farther down the road.

What is down this road? Malcom wants to go; I can feel it in the way he looks at us. We're both too tired. Like we're half asleep.

I catch myself following a little close when I get like this. The driver in front of me keeps flashing his brakes and slowing down dramatically. He's fucking jumpy really. Who the fuck does that? I know they are out there but one less doesn't mean much. Just get a bigger car asshole. We hit a green light on Moreno Avenue, so I gun it through the intersection and rip around the slow poke while I look straight ahead. Lay into the gas a little to make it sting his pride. I love the way this feels. We're almost clear of him when a Walker hits our hood and rolls up and over the top of the car. Look at him, a real no-brained streetdrooler. I wiggle the car back and forth a little to make sure he clears the bike racks up top. Looking over my shoulder I see him stand back up in the street. Aw. Only worth 10 points. I depress the windshield wiper & hoodflush button. Bella's eyes flutter a little but she continues to rest. Poor baby. How much better she has it than me and Malcom when we were kids though.


I stood back up.

"My name is Malcom, Malcom Mama!" I stood taller then. Malcom.

"Why do you make me do this?" She swings again.

I felt something growing around my left eye socket. She wasn't gonna win this time in her long billed Goofy hat with those flapping ears and all those times I said nothing. When she connects again I realize that I can't blink. Fuck it, I won't blink. The dented primer white minivan and the two car seats and the man in the driver seat mama "wrestles with" all be damned.

"Hey." A white man wearing an army back pack shouts at mama. Mama and I stare at him. She grabs me and pushes me into the side door, and I go on autopilot. Mama doesn't break eye contact with the man. I'm stuck over the busted spring on the front bench where I get a good look at the back of mama's bucket seat. I'm seven. Rotor blades spin over us flying map of the earth: oh dark thirty jerky extraction from a hot landing zone. I'm thirty seven. Broken bathroom mirror at the apartment, Jen screaming, holding me, wrapping my bleeding knuckles, I am thirty nine, an auto mechanic narrowly dodging the 220 volt shock every day. I'm a well-grounded motherfucker. I'm 41, just home from work.

"My name is Malcom, Malcom." I slide the contact in by feel, check the mirror to make sure my eyes are clear and that I am still me. Malcom. My Prius kicks off her combustion engine. Goddamned gas guzzler- especially since I installed that cattle catcher on the front bumper. Gas maybe cheap but shows we come from the ghetto. We get the weirdest looks when we drive through the wire to the north side of town to Bella's school. North-side where electricity is free. We will move there when our credit clears and the VA finally comes through. Hell they own me, so for now it's just our two bedrooms with a common bathroom on the wrong side of the concertina.

Jen is upstairs. I can see her through the bars from here, sitting in my car. Normally I like watching her, just for a few minutes after work, seeing her up there calms me down. Tonight, she's looking out the living room window wreathed in our Christmas lights. It's late. Like two. She doesn't see me, the lights are on behind her. She's pissed. Rough day with Bella. We have been trying to get her to behave normally but talk just doesn't work with that girl. She just sits in her room and reads. She's seven. Wears glasses if you sit on her to do it. I think she takes them off at school because what she needs she can see just a foot from her face. Long after lights-out she's camped out reading under the covers by the glow from her cellphone. Our bookworm Bella. No wonder she's a target for bullying. I've seen the shiners.

I lean the seat back to give myself some time to think. I've had a ring in the glove box for a month, but there is never time. Jen, she's tough but good. Met her in the Blood and the Suck. Seen her carry her weight in gear. She once punched a shovel clean through a man's jaw. Wiggling. Stood over the fallen. Broken teeth, detached fingers. Forget. My contact bunches, folding into the right upper corner of my eye socket. I ignore it. Fuck. I check that my knife is still locked in its black sheath and pocket the ring from my glove box.

The milk white stairs are uneven and the safety grip-tape is coming up from the bent nail boards. Damn civie landlord. Everything's painted in vintage orange peel here. Door's unlocked, again. Jen has one eye open on the couch watching the video feed from our computer monitor. Even from the doorway I can see her skin has become yellow and saggy under the once smooth mocha. I know that kind of tired. Here's Bella's ball cap. Too bad her dad doesn't visit.

I've given up trying to leave them. The wounds on my knuckles may never close from being banged by turning wrenches but I will do right by them. It's the only thing I haven't fucked up. I make the rounds through the house turning off the hall and kitchen lights. We dim into the Christmas glow. A few packages. Bella's ball cap on the table. Home. Jen opens up her other eye, no longer conserving her night vision. She's always on point even years out of the bush.

"Hon, why do you always look at me like that?"

"What are you watching?" I say as I sit down beside her.

Three minutes pass. Grainy vid images flicker old men dick around a psych-ward.

"Jack Nicholson. Cuckoo's Nest. Let me see your hands."

"They're fine Jen. I got something I want to talk with you about." I slowly slide down the couch and kneel in front of her, laying my head in her lap. How many times have I been here just after Bella goes to bed, looking for a little action? But for this, I just don't know how to ask her. I don't know how to stay. I run my hand lightly on the outside of her thigh. Jen's hand floats down and brushes my hair from behind my ear, but no words can come out of me. I can't look up. She'll see.

"It's ok. She's been asleep since four this afternoon hon. I drew a bath for us but it's gone cold by now."

I lay a little longer to feel the reassuring heat in her hand. It's time.

"Jen, I want to-"

The door opens down the hall.


"Bella?"

The poor thing walks into the living room looking sleep lost. I can see she has sweated clear through her pee-jays even though she was fine at 11 when I checked in on her last. Malcom looks uncomfortable, maybe he thought he was going to get some to-night. My baby doesn't say anything but just comes over beside me on the couch. She leans against me and I can feel the heat coming off her skin.

"wu vew nuh-oh nuh-oh," Bella gurgles.

Malcom looks sharply up from my lap at me. I make eye con-tact with him and almost a minute goes by. He's calculating something. I can't tell what. He's got that look he used to get during a long patrol. Bella gurgles again, and I feel tears. My tears. She's so hot. Malcom's neck tightens and he shakes once very hard like a hammer recoiling from a railroad spike. Draw-ing his shoulders back tight. Mommy. I lean my head slightly over to her and put my arm around her shoulders. I don't know what to do. Bella begins to shriek and tremble: I hold her tighter. Mommy. Too tight. I reach down to her wrists and pull Bella between Malcom and me, facing me. Look at me. Mommy. Mal-com stands up. Bella's eyes widen and she looks terrified. Bella lunges at me with her mouth, but Malcom grabs her wrists and holds her at arms-length from me. Mommy.

Malcom twists Bella roughly by the arms away from me pinning her on my couch.

"What the fuck are you doing Mal?"

Look at me. Holding her arms down with his knees he begins to draw open Bella's eyes with his fingers like he is looking for something caught in them.

"What's wrong with my baby?"

"What's your name Bella? Bella?" Malcom is crying but he's crushing her. Look at me.

I slap him. Slap him. Slap. Pound his back. Bella is struggling to breathe. Baby. Look at me. I slug him hard in the left eye. Look at me. Malcom rears up and I know something is wrong because he's ready to hit me too. Bella leaps from the couch and claws into the meat of Malcom's neck. Blood springs. Too much. Much too much. An Incident.

"Jen. Get the ice. We have to stop her fever." We both look down at his Bouie knife strapped to his thigh.

I know, Malcom. Look at what she did to your neck. I might have to break yours, too. Baby. I can't do it. Baby. I stare at his contact on the shag rug as he drags Bella down the hallway by an arm and a flailing leg toward the bathroom.

"Ayl wu vee Ayms are reAyms are nuh-oh nuh-oh,"


Hot Love you no no they are pushing me into the water. I keep reaching out to burning them I love you I'm sorry I'm sorry no no. I'm so hungry burning. There is a way that red light shimmers through falling water when you are looking up from under the spigot of a white porcelain tub. Red. They keep grabbing too hot my wrists. Hungry. Dumping devils ice cubes and I keep reaching out like snow angels we made and the smell it's like lilacs I always loved the lavender smells of meat her bath towels and the rubber scalding ducks eat and the mechanical goldfishes

I read it takes 3 minutes bite and 37 seconds I ask the snowan-
gels please please where my body is and I can see please bite
everything for miles up snap through the ceiling the knife in
my neck angels are singing I'm reaching out I'm sorry I'm sorry
know I love you mommy and I keep reaching and they are pushing me down please please inside the dark dark red hunger.

# JAKE AND LEROY HAD A FIGHT

## JIM DOERING

On a dusty parking lot behind an old honky-tonk west of Shreveport, Jake Cameron took one last puff on his Winston and threw it down at the feet of his best friend. Love-sick Blues by Hank Williams played inside as he said, "Leroy St. James, if you say one more word, I'm gonna hitcha' again. Got it?"

Leroy's face showed a cheery smile even though he felt terrible inside. The blood from Jake's punch was oozing a bit from the corner of his mouth, but it didn't hurt too much. He licked the blood off with the tip of his tongue, but the smile remained frozen on his face.

"I mean it, Leroy. I swear to God. I don't care if you're my last friend on this good green earth, ya' say one more goddamned thing 'bout her and I will lay you out like an undertaker on a battlefield."

Leroy stared straight ahead and said nothing. Instead, he turned and ambled toward the back door of the bar, wiping his bleeding mouth on the right sleeve of his black snap-front shirt. Leroy got hit for speaking the truth about Jake's wife cheating on him. By telling, he'd shoved a dagger deep into his buddy's heart. They'd exchanged punches and Leroy prayed that would be the end of it between them. But it wasn't.

Leroy turned and gave one last look to the fella who'd been his best friend since second grade and shrugged his shoulders. Then he threw open the spring-closed screen door and went inside. By the time it slammed loudly behind him, he was already at the beaten-up bar, slinging down the lukewarm dregs of his Jack and Coke. He signaled the barkeep and yelled at him, "Gimme a double and keep 'em comin'."

Jake waited outside, wondering if Leroy would dare come back. When he figured everything was said and done, he walked around the shabby building to the front lot, where his rusty, two-toned, '71 Chevy pick-up was parked. The night was warm; the air moist and heavy. Jake took off his sweat-stained trucker's hat and flipped it through the open window. The hat landed on the grey cloth-covered bench seat and he wiped his eyes with the back of his hand, wondering what in the hell he was gonna do. Sweat and maybe a little something else clouded his vision. The old truck door groaned in agony as he got in. Jake was angry and confused. He knew he had to get home, but he had no idea what he'd do when he got there.

Jake started the engine up, stuck the shifter on the steering column into drive and hit the gas hard. The back wheels sprayed a cloud of rocks and dirt on the beaters and trucks around him. The dusty haze hid the vehicle's dim red taillights as he sped out of the parking lot laying rubber. On the road, Jake tasted metal in his mouth. He turned to his left and spit the remainder of the fight and what was left of his pride out the driver's side window.

Back in the bar, Leroy couldn't forget what had just happened, even if he got blind, stinking drunk and passed out in a puddle of his own puke and piss. Instead, he turned and asked a worn-around-the-edges bottle-blonde wearing a red gingham blouse with a too-short denim skirt if she cared to dance. 'Diggy Liggy Lo' by Doug Kershaw played on the jukebox, and the blonde's eyes lit up as she said yes. Maybe she'd even want a little company after the music stopped.

Jake sped down a winding two lane road headed for the Texas line. It was gonna be three in the morning before he got home to the little two bedroom bungalow he and Marigold shared. If you'd asked him yesterday, he would've told you he loved her more than life itself. But not tonight.

After thirty minutes of bouncing down the deteriorated state highway, Jake Cameron started to chuckle. A laugh began low and slow and didn't stop until his belly hurt. When Friday night started, he had a wife, a best friend, and a pocket full of money from a just-cashed paycheck. Three hours later he had nothing left to show for any of it. His life had turned into the punch-line from every craptastic country song he'd ever heard. Maybe his daddy was right; when life started to go south on ya, it could turn to shit faster than a stray dog eating spoiled food from a dumped-over garbage can.

Jake twisted the cheap plastic knob of the Delco radio and scanned the dial looking for some music to keep him company. Zydeco bellowed from the speaker in the dash. He reached into the glove box hoping to find a pint of cheap whiskey stashed there earlier in the week, but his hand felt something else. Jake smiled as he grabbed it from under the pile of papers. He set the thing on the seat and continued searching for the hooch.

Feeling around, he located the mostly full glass bottle, quickly unscrewed the metal cap, and took a long, hard pull. It burned something fierce going down. Holding the bottle and the steering wheel with his left hand, he lit a cigarette with his right and glanced at his unexpected find. Remy must have left it there when he borrowed the truck and forgotten to take it back. Jake stared at the blue-black metal; it glinted in the dashboard lights. Reaching across the seat, he picked up the worn, fully loaded .38 revolver. He took another swig of rotgut as a ball of anger itching to explode swelled inside of him. It started in his gut and climbed all the way up into his throat. Jake turned up the music, edged down on the gas and held the gun tight. An idea had bored its way into his skull. Finally, he had a plan.

# KEYS

## BARCLAY JONES

It's a new bed. We got it right after we married. We were stoked: it was our first real bed. We'd been in California for almost a year and had spent the whole time sleeping on a shitty full-sized mattress and box spring sitting right on the floor. You get used to having backaches sleeping like that.

This bed sits up high. My feet don't even touch the floor when I sit on the edge, like I am right now.

This is the biggest room we've ever had. Far bigger than the walk in closet we slept in at our last place. Funny thing, the size of the room didn't really bother us; what drove us crazy was not having a closet.

This room is big enough to have a chair and table across from the bed. I thought about sitting there instead. But then I would be facing away from the door. I really want to face the door. I see my hand shake, reaching for the glass of water on the nightstand, as I sit and wait for her. She always walks straight to the bedroom when she comes home. She likes to hang her clothes, then sit and breathe for a minute or two before going back out to our hectic household.

We have roommates, the same ones we had before we got married. Nothing changed after we got married, though everyone kept saying it would. Everyone always says that, but no one can ever explain it. The day after our wedding it all felt the same, even the roommates.

We went on like that for a while, thinking nothing had changed. Then her dad died.

Everything changed.

Our roommates were everywhere. Claiming our own privacy was weird; we were being reclusive, our friends didn't know what to do. None of us could afford to be on our own. We were young and poor and just wanted to be free; instead we were shackled to each other and our collective shortcomings. None of us knew what to do. I didn't know how to comfort her. Our roommates didn't know what to say, they just wanted her grieving to be over so they could stop feeling inadequate. We wanted them to go.

Our big spacious home felt cramped. We shared each other's drama and began to hate each other for it. Little things like toilet seats and dirty dishes. Hell, even this morning, one of my roommates, my best friend even, lost his keys. No one could find them. I left the earliest and was at work already when I got the call about his keys. I could hear everyone in the background looking. My wife, grieving, had to take him to work.

Lost keys; something so simple can bring into such sharp relief how much better it would be to be married and alone. Alone together so we can live life, love each other and deal with our grief, instead of someone else's missing property.

The room darkens as dusk crowds out the day. The blinds are up and the light is off. I leave it that way. The house is quiet, a rare moment, and I sit and listen to the sinking, creaking noises of an old house as it stretches and groans into the night.

She's late. Again. This time because she has to pick up my roommate, the one who lost his keys. I can hear my breath as I sit and wait. The dim gray light escapes into night and the room slips into darkness.

I sit and wait for her. Listening to my own breath and the quiet jingle of my roommate's keys I found under the sheets of our new bed.

# TALES OF THE PINK WALRUS AND THE WONDERLAND VAN ESCAPE

## SPIDER MCQUEEN

It sure would feel good to take a shower right now and sooth the fresh scars on my legs, I thought. If only I could get this snoring, sweaty pink walrus of a man off me and my eight-thousand dollar tits. As I lay beneath the oily drops of his sweat, something clicked inside the center of my mind, like a cooking timer twisted all the way to the beginning, come back around and hit the buzzer. At that moment I knew what had been left of my soul was finally gone.

In the wee early morning hours, after an agonizing night of flatulence and a variety of snoring patterns, he finally moved enough to allow me to escape from underneath him. I scrambled from his grasp and snatched up my gold and leopard print Coach bag sitting on the empty dresser of the hotel room, cut a right into the bathroom and flicked on the light. The ventilation fan began to hum when the lights came on so I quietly shut the door so as to not disturb the snore pattern of Mr. Pink Walrus as he lay spread eagle and naked on the messy king-size bed.

Yuck, I thought to myself as I took one last glance at the abomination that once sprawled between my legs. I managed to keep down the previous night's dinner as I held the door knob long enough to shut the door without a sound.

After attempting to shake away the memory, I draped a towel over the long bathroom sink and pulled out the contents of my kit, one by one for accountability, and placed them gently onto the soft surface I had made:

1. A clean mirror kept safe inside a velvet Crown Royal bag.

2. A beverage straw... cut in half.

3. A voided credit card.

4. A hollowed-out vial of lipstick stuffed with the finest Floridian cocaine.

I tapped the vial onto the compact mirror, and the white crumbles spread out like coarse salt onto their own reflection. I crushed and separated two thick lines of breakfast cheer. Just then, as if by magic, my phone vibrated inside my purse. It was probably Frieda checking up on me again.

How did she even know I was up this early?

Women's intuition perhaps?

"I'll have to call her later," I thought to myself.

I leaned over with my handy straw and snorted both lines...one for each nostril. The chemicals hit my brain with a jolt causing me to stand straight up like a dick on Viagra. I leaned my head back and let the juice run down my throat.

Gross, but afterwards... very nice.

The phone vibrated again. This time I searched throughout my bag, found it and answered before she hung up.

"Yeah...?" I whispered so as to not wake the monstrosity lying in bed in the other room.

"Hey, Retard!" Frieda blared on the other end of the line.

"Wait a second," I whispered again and turned down the volume on my phone, "Yeah, what's up, Shit-bag?"

"I'm calling to see if you needed a ride, Bitch." she exclaimed jokingly in between the perpetual smacks of her chewing gum.

"What the fuck are you doing up so early?" I whispered back.

"I never slept." Frieda snorted. "Sleep is for the sober. Do you want a ride or what?"

"Yeah, come get me," I grabbed a bar of hotel soap from the sink and scanned the label. "I'm at the Continental on Biscayne. I'm walking out now."

"Alright, I'll call you when I get there. Meet me out front...and show some titty like a good girl." Frieda laughed as she popped a bubble in my sensitive eardrum.

"You're a trip. I'll see you soon." I hung up and packed all my shit in my Crown Royal bag. No need to shower. I'll redeem my-self after I've gone home and counted all this money I made last night. Of course, I was naked and dirty enough to make use of the shower facilities at hand, but it was still dark and early. I'd find my dress and get the fuck out of there before I had to force small talk with a man I hoped to never see again.

I don't do small talk.

With my bag tucked under my arm, I turned off the light and slowly opened the door to the bedroom. I glanced out of the panoramic window at the early morning darkness and started a timer in my head. How long before the sun would come up, and how long I had to get out of this disaster scene.

Mr. Pink Walrus stirred a little, but his snoring was consistent as he lay there like a rotisserie chicken on the ruffled sheets. His terrible mouth hung open and leaked saliva against his poor, helpless pillow. For a moment, I stood there as if staring into a lava lamp, wondering how a person could ever let themselves go like that. I was caught in a surrealistic daze as I watched him struggle to breathe beneath the weight of his massive rolls and his pinkish-white flesh. It solidified the shocking fact that I had no limitations to my bed partners as long as they had no limitations to their bank account. I tore myself away from this startling self-realization, and scanned the room for my slip of a dress. It's a shitty shame I hardly remember even wearing a dress after a night of drinking at the hotel bar.

Fuck! Where was it? Did I come up here naked? Then I saw it, peeking out from underneath his massive left man-boob.

I knew right then, there was absolutely no fucking way that I was going home with that dress. I scanned the room for an alternative piece of clothing I could wear that would get me past the concierge without suspicion. The only thing I saw was Pink Walrus's large navy blazer hanging neatly over the chair by the desk. The jacket was huge; the shoulder span easily cleared the outline of the chair entirely and looked as if it were standing upright on its own. I tiptoed to the desk where his laptop rested and slid it into my bag before wrapping his blazer around my body like a burrito. My heels were under his side of the bed. I mourned their loss and slipped out of the room, quietly closed the door and made a serious beeline to the stairwell at the end of the elegantly-carpeted hall.

I fell into a dim stairwell, the walls dotted with sconce lighting. Classical music filled the closed-in space. Clutching tightly to my beautiful Coach bag, I ran a marathon down the seven flights of stairs while barely producing an echo. There was no way I could have run that fast down the stairs in heels. I was glad I left him my cheap shoes as a reminder to never leave expensive shit out the morning after paying for sex.

Sadly, the door at the bottom of the stairs led to the equally elegant and carpeted four-star lobby instead of the parking lot I was more appropriately dressed for. I mentally prepared to walk past the front desk as casually as I could. Forget the fact that I was naked, barefoot and swallowed-up inside a man's blazer seven times my size.

Perhaps my personality would pull it off, I thought jokingly.

I leaned against the door inside the stairwell and pulled out my phone to call Frieda.

No answer.

I dialed again. This time the phone went straight to voicemail.

Fucking perfect.

I was NOT going to spend a whole lot of time waiting outside a four-star hotel looking like I escaped a violent rape scene.

I mean, I *was* a prostitute... but that didn't mean I had to look like the crack variety. God only knew what my hair looked like after being pinned beneath Jabba the Hutt for three hours.

My phone read 6:15 A.M.

The sun might not be up just yet.

Perhaps I could slip past the front doors into the early morning darkness undetected and meet Frieda in the parking lot somewhere... if she picked up her goddamn phone.

Adrenaline began to mix with the cocaine in my bloodstream, causing my heartbeat to speed up even faster than usual. I grabbed the doorknob to the lobby and took one last deep breath. I was prepared to strut when my phone vibrated again and nearly put me in cardiac arrest. The number was from an unknown caller. Frieda was known to call from a payphone if her disposable cell phone ran out of minutes so I assumed the best and answered on the second ring.

"Goddammit, Frieda...!" I whispered as loudly as a whisper could be and still be called a whisper. "Where in the *fuck* are you?"

"Ginger?" replied the just-waking voice of the animal from upstairs. "Is this Ginger from last night?"

I hung up quickly. How did Pink Walrus get my number? What was I *thinking* to give this fool my *real* number anyway? I couldn't have been THAT drunk?

Then again, I very well might have. According to record, I quite possibly could have been wasted out of my fucking mind last night... ESPECIALLY to have given up my REAL cell phone number to a random stranger whom I intended to never see again.

Lesson learned, you stupid bitch.

I sighed and proceeded to powerwalk through the elegant lobby; my eyes dead-set on the clear glass doors that led past the elegant grand piano and outside to valet parking. I prayed Frieda didn't get pulled over or something.

I brushed past the piano to my left, past the eyes glaring at me from the business section in the seating area by the cobblestone fireplace to my right...past the long marble front desk where the lady behind it took one look at me and knew that I wasn't a part of the group.

"Miss?" She called out to a half-naked woman who blatantly ignored her while hauling some serious ass toward the fabulously-designed exit doors. She then grabbed the phone, presumably to alert some type of authority to my apparent thievery and solicitation. My bare feet moved quickly past the automatic glass doors, out into the windy drizzle of the morning.

It was beginning to rain.

Thanks again, Florida!

Frieda's burgundy conversion van was nowhere in sight as I scanned the empty valet parking area that began to dot with droplets of rain from the coming storm.

"Miss?" I heard a male voice call from behind me. I didn't even waste time turning around to see where it came from before I took off into the parking lot littered with expensive sedans and luxury convertibles. My bare feet slapped against the cold, wet asphalt as quickly as a girl hopped-up on stimulants could go. I crouched between cars and squinted through the rain for the closest way to the free shuttle across Biscayne Boulevard just in case Frieda decided to change her mind and ditch me. I cursed under my breath at my tardy roommate. It wouldn't be the first time she had let me down after all.

I figured there was absolutely no way I had time to call and cuss her out properly until I made it to the train where the rain wouldn't ruin my recently-purchased touchscreen phone, so I focused my concentration on the most tactful of escape methods. My heart was pumping so fast inside my chest anyways that I didn't see the point in calling Frieda unless she brought the ambulance with her. My hair began to stick to my face and I wiped it away with my free hand while maintaining a death-grip on my Coach bag with the other as I strained to see which direction I was to haul ass in.

The phone vibrated inside my bag.

This time I was too terrified to answer it.

I had to get the hell out of this parking lot before I was caught. God only knew how many surveillance cameras were hiding in the bushes and on the street lamps due to the hotel's upscale status. I took off without thinking towards the sound of the morning traffic onto the sidewalk at Biscayne Boulevard. I felt the eyes of every last driver in Miami on that busy street as they passed. I almost knew what they were thinking; seeing an unkempt and obviously naked woman covered in a burlap sack of an expensive man's blazer. I tried to ignore the sounds of honking and catcalls from the traffic. My foot came down on a piece of broken beer bottle, and I felt the blood immediately begin to flow out of my body and onto the sidewalk, marking my path.

I had to get off the sidewalk with bare feet. What was I thinking? This is Miami, for shit's sake!

Luckily, Bayside Park spread out for about a mile on my right. I plucked the glass out of my heel without missing a beat and proceeded to fumble around in my purse for the phone that was now vibrating constantly.

Scanning the park for a tree to stand under and wait without being completely drenched by the increasing rainfall, I finally gathered enough courage to answer the phone.

"Stank-Pussy!" She half-whispered jokingly. She was hardly ever mature about anything, "There's cops pulling up and shit. I know it was you, Bitch. Did you rob a bank too?"

I loathed her humor in situations where I needed someone to be focused and serious.

"I'm at the park already." I said," I thought I was gonna have to catch a cab waiting for you."

"You oughta be glad I called you this morning, Hoe-Bag!" My loving partner in crime replied, her gum popping in my ear. "Okay, I'm gonna get the fuck out of this sketchy-ass parking lot and back onto Biscayne. Stay on the phone till I see you. I'll follow the trail of herpes on the sidewalk."

"Oh my God, fuck you!"

She laughed so hard, she honked through her nose like a duck.

"What the fuck happened anyways?" she asked after she finally finished laughing at my expense.

"I'll tell you when we get back to the house… just hurry." I pleaded desperately, "By the way, I'm really hating you right now…"

Cradling the phone between my shoulder and my wet face, I quickly searched through my bag, found my cigarettes and popped one between my lips. I spotted a tree to stand beneath and limped over to it as my foot-blood colored the grass. Annoyed at how my morning was materializing, I finally pulled out a working lighter and attempted to shield the flame beneath the huge blazer to light my cancer stick despite the unfortunate weather. The smoke in my lungs calmed me down a bit and stopped my heart from racing. I stood around watching the homeless fail miserably as they tried to get out of the rain.

"Alright, I'm out of the parking lot and back on Biscayne headed toward Bayside." Frieda declared, "Tell me you went that direction."

I nodded before I realized she couldn't see me. I took another drag before I confirmed that she was indeed headed in the right direction.

"I'm walking in the grass now, away from the sidewalk." I told her between drags of my cigarette. "I learned my lesson from walking on the fucking sidewalk without shoes. Cut my foot pretty bad."

"Well, where's your goddamn shoes?" Frieda asked matter-of-factly.

I pulled in more smoke from the slowly dampening cigarette and scanned the traffic for her large, sketchy van. "I don't see you yet..." I replied, ignoring the question. Then I saw her. The large, red conversion van with the HELLA fog-lights on top held up the traffic as my amateur rescuer careened to get to the far right of the street without any thought of a turn signal. I sighed and flicked the burning embers into the rain.

"I see you." I waved in her direction. "Here I come."

Hanging up the phone, I hobbled toward the curbside van as quickly as I could before she could hold up any more traffic. Both of her front windows were rolled all the way down despite the rain.

"Hey, Ho!" Frieda smiled with wild abandon, her voice barely audible over the rain that was getting heavier and heavier with every second. I opened the passenger-side door and jumped in just as she sped off down the street, nearly knocking me off balance.

"Cunt!" I shouted angrily and slammed the door. She laughed maniacally in response and made a quick left onto Flagler Street toward our shared motel room in Little Havana.

I hung my feet out the window and let the rain lick my wounds.

Fuck the seats.

# THE ALCHEMIST

## DONALD GEORGE LOSEY

N o one wants you to do the things you're doing," she said, arms crossed, leaning against his porch railing. He nodded, thinking that if she'd known the plank supporting her had been only a twig three months ago she wouldn't have been so condescending. But then again, it probably wouldn't matter. Everything he did was eclipsed by the crocodiles. He lit a cigarette with a match that had once been a toothpick. As he smoked he tapped his thumb restlessly against the filter. It almost made her smile; he never could stay completely still.

"You know, part of me still cares for you," she said slowly, sounding unsure. "I-I'm not sure why I brought that up-"

"To soften the blow," he said.

She put her hand lightly to her temple. "But the crocodiles, why?"

"Do you have any idea how much work I put into them? I have to start with green beans, then newts, then komodos. Do you know how hard it is to turn a vegetable into a lizard? No one's ever come close to that."

A newt passed between her feet and she cringed. "Because no one can do what you can." She laughed, "I mean come on, it should be impossible. For everyone else, it is, but for you, it isn't. Which is why it's so preposterous, you've got this amazing gift, and you squander it on crocodiles. Making goddamn crocodiles. No one wants more crocodiles. Can't you see that? Who even likes crocodiles?"

"I do." He flicked his spent cigarette over her shoulder. A passing komodo stopped and eyed it suspiciously, cocked its head sideways, then ate it. "Plenty of people do," he too crossed his arms over his chest hoping she'd notice he was mocking her.

She leaned forward, jutted out her chin. "Name one, I dare you. Name one person."

"Herpetologists."

"What?"

"People who study lizards. They wouldn't study them if they didn't like them."

Her shoulders slumped. "Other than someone who gets paid to study them."

"Do you know how much a herpetologist makes? Not much. They don't do it for the pay."

She sighed, long, slow, and deliberate. "You're being intentionally thick."

"Do you know how thick a croc's skin is? They're like the tanks of the animal kingdom."

"I'm leaving."

"No. You're staying." He pushed his front door open a few inches, "have a drink, old times' sake."

"No, I'm leaving. You never listen."

"Couldn't the same be said about you?"

The wind picked up, sending a fallen leaf skidding across the porch between them.

She dropped her hands to her sides. "I don't know what you mean. I'm the only person that ever listened to you. I'm the only one who ever tried to make sense out of-" she indicated his yard, the lizards, the bean stalks "-all this."

He nodded. "You did, that's true. You listened. You tried. Past tense. You don't anymore."

She was silent for a moment. She sized him up again. In stature he looked the same as always, too tall, too thin, but there was something new, something that had been growing ever since she left him. It was just now visible. He wouldn't meet her eyes. Absentmindedly he began to scratch his neck with one finger. He turned his head, looked at her SUV in his gravel driveway. Weeds sprouted up around its tires.

"Are you getting out much?"

His finger stopped short just under his chin. He shrugged lightly, "does it look like it?"

"No."

"You're right. I'm not. I'm busy."

Two newts, their green backs shining in the sunlight, scurried across the porch and through his still open door. An involuntary shiver ran up her spine.

"I'm leaving," she said. "Try to take care of yourself though, okay?"

# BELLE DE JOUR

## BRICE EZELL

As the sand warms its way between my toes and the crashing of the waves forms a steady, lulling rhythm, I take in the solitude that but an hour ago seemed impossible. Finally, I've found a place where I can avoid thinking about my mother. In designing the beach house, she created a shrine to all of the memories she manufactured, the ones she was actually thousands of miles away from. Only the shores of the beach were free from her reach. I avoid this place when my mom is gone, but the circumstances being as they are I agreed to come back. She could have just flown into D.C., but Dad was particularly insistent on her coming to the beach house instead. Maybe Dad's just trying to make sure we haven't forgotten what Mom is like after this long year and a half. I remember the phone calls he'd make, the ones where he tried to pretend like everything was normal. Those were never long conversations.

This is the longest she's been gone since I was in high school. She made sure to tell us on the few phone calls she could afford that this was "really important" and that she wouldn't ever be gone unless it was "absolutely necessary." But as smart as she is, my mother forgets that over the years, the distance has left me desensitized. Whoever it is she works for is obviously unaware of what it feels like to be lied to for twenty-seven years; otherwise, they would have stopped wasting time explaining a long time ago. At least they've got my dad and my sister.

She's coming back tonight. I don't know what I'm going to say to her. I know I'll probably cave and join in the familial joy at her return, but I shouldn't. I look back at the house and see my sister overlooking the beach, trying to look like she isn't spying on me. Loving as they are, they never know when to give up.

Dinner's on in five minutes or so, because, "big surprise," Mom's arriving late. I want to yell back at her that they can start eating without me, but it's better to avoid the battle. I walk up the beach, the last fragments of sunlight fading from the sand behind me. Kara looks at me as I walk up, with that classic smile of hers.

"Dinner's on soon," she says.

"I heard."

"Mom'll be back—

"Sometime in the unknown future, I know. Do I need to do anything?"

Her smile fades a little. "No, Dad and I got everything. Ed?"

"Yes?"

"Could you just... try and be happy for the kids? They're excited, and they'll be worried if you aren't."

I clap the sand out of my flip-flops loudly and feign a smile. "Sure. Anything for the kids."

To most, the beach house would look just like any other vacation spot, but anyone who knew my mother would see that it was an extension of her more than anything. She never kept scrapbooks, partly because she didn't have the time, but mostly because she didn't need to. The beach house was the architectural incarnation of my mother's idealized family. Any time we had friends over they pointed out the same things. "It's so cozy!"

"You all must be really close!" "Look how the kids have grown up!" My mom is the happiest in those moments, the ones where everything looks perfect. My father made sure that when she was gone, nothing changed here. He came once a month, arranging everything according to her unspoken specifications. He used to ask Kara and me for help; sometimes Kara goes, but he gave up on calling me a long time ago.

I always joked that many historians don't go to the lengths Mom did to preserve our picturesque family, but that never stopped her. Some photography dates as recently as Kara's wedding, and many of the crayon scribblings go back as early as my preschool years. We're here collectively for about a month every year, but it feels more like our home than our house in D.C. does.

I throw open the double screen door, noticing a slight chill in the house. *Dad's forgotten to turn up the thermostat.* Walking into the kitchen, I hear my father telling Kara's youngest, Elise, a story that I knew too well. She was sitting on his lap, looking up eagerly at his wrinkled face.

"...so your grandmother and I, we had a whole week on the beaches of France to do whatever we wanted. Do you want to know what we did?"

"Tell me Grampa! Tell me!"

"Well, we ate all of the French food that we could. That's how I got my big belly," he said. He hits his gut hard with the palm of his hand, causing Elise to giggle. "A lot of cheese, and a delicious dessert called *crème puffs*. You ever had a *crème puff* before?"

"No. What are they like?"

"Well, they're the tastiest thing you'll ever eat. You should ask your grandmother about it when she gets here. She'd love to make you some."

"Did you have dessert the whole time in France?"

"No, but I wish we did. We had some great French bread, plenty of cheese, and some really delicious veal. You know, France is where I came up with the little name I call your grandmother."

"You mean sweetie?"

Dad laughs. "No, not sweetie. But that is a name I call her often, you're right. No, it came one night when your grandmother and I were eating at a restaurant right by the ocean. There was a man there playing the guitar, he was a Spanish musician. He played a love song that was absolutely beautiful. He was from Spain, but he spoke French just as good as a French person. When your grandmother went to go to the bathroom, I walked up to the musician and asked him about the song. He said it was called 'Belle de Jour.' You know what that means?"

"Grampa, I don't speak French!"

"Oh, that's right. Well, it means 'Beauty of the Day.' And I thought to myself, 'Well, what better way to describe your grandmother than that?' When we went walking on the beach later that night, I told her that she was my *belle de jour*. That's been my name for her ever since."

She stays silent for a few moments, absentmindedly staring at her fingernails the way kids do. "You're cute, Grampa."

Dad laughs loudly, slapping his knee in an exaggerated way. He leans in and kisses her on the cheek. "Well thank you dear. But I have to say, I think you and your mom are a lot cuter than I am."

"I don't know Dad," Kara says, taking Elise from his lap. "I think Elise is *way* cuter than I am."

"Mommy is pretty," Elise says.

"Why thank you honey. Just wait 'till Gramma gets back tonight. She's even prettier than I am."

I throw the rag I was using to brush the sand off my legs into the sink, and walk out of the room.

The hallway that led to my room was conveniently the one my mother had decided to line with family photographs. When she brought guests over, she always drew their attention to the pictures with all four of us. That was difficult since she's maybe in a fifth of them, but she always had a way of guiding people around so it seemed we were spending every other weekend soaking in the sun, smiling like a family on a Hallmark card. But without even looking, I can feel her absence in those old pictures. As I begin to walk faster down the hallway, a hand suddenly clasps my arm.

Kara spins me around. "Could you just be happy? I know you've heard that a million times, but it's a cute story."

"A 'cute' story? Am I the only one who remembers why Dad's romantic getaway to France even happened?"

"Of course not—"

"Dad got to go on that trip after begging to see mom after six months of no communication at all. Is that bit lost on you?"

"No—"

"And, let's not forget that sweet, romantic story is the only thing we know about that trip. Because 'they' made Dad keep his mouth shut about the whole thing."

"I haven't forgotten, Ed. I've forgiven."

"Are you not bothered..." I lower my voice, "...even slightly by how Dad pretends that our past has been a goddamn storybook? It's mostly been a lot of grainy, long-distance phone calls, Christmases with an empty place setting, and a hell of a lot of regret. Can we at least acknowledge that we've struggled?"

"What good would that do?"

"Right, 'what good would that do?' God forbid we ever question for a second Mom's loyalty to an institution that's done nothing but fuck us over ever since we were kids."

"Does this argument have to come up tonight? Tonight?"

"Right, 'cause I'm just supposed to be happy that she's home? I'm just supposed to push past the fact that she'll walk through that door without anything to tell us, yet again. Just another little secret to keep us safe from, you know, some vaguely defined threat. She'll probably tell Dad, because for some reason he gets clearance to know all her shit. But us, nah, we don't make any sacrifices. Why should we get to know anything?"

She folds her arms. "You know, I think we'll start dinner without you."

"Good."

I hope Dad hadn't heard all of that, though if I thought he would empathize with me, I would have told him straight to his face. I turn and walk toward my room, moving faster to avoid my mother's gaze through the frames. From the kitchen I faintly hear Dad ask where I am. I pick up the pace; I don't want to hear Kara's excuse. But as I pass by my parents' bedroom, I stop.

The one rule that was drilled into me when I was young was that I was never to enter my parents' bedroom unless asked. The only time I ever tried was when I was six. I was trying to figure out where Mom was, as I hadn't yet understood the gravity of her job. Though a child's yearning motivated my desire, my father punished me like an inmate at Abu Ghraib. Back then I thought the red mark left by the belt would be there forever. For all my misdemeanors in my adolescence, whether smoking weed in my room or totaling my dad's Jeep, I never experienced anything like what happened after that excursion into my parents' room.

Looking back down the hall, I can hear the clanging of spoons on ceramic dishes; dinner's being served. *They know I would never try to look into Mom's room.* I quietly test the handle and it's unlocked. Staring at the entrance to the kitchen, I slowly turn the handle, coughing loudly as the latch clicks. I quickly get into the room and close the door behind me.

The moment the door shuts I instantly feel how flat the air is in the room. My pulse began racing when I snuck in, but it doesn't feel like the secret labyrinth I had imagined. All the lights are off, as is the A/C; it's a wonder Dad could sleep at all in this room. The furniture is faded, as if it hadn't been replaced in thirty-five years. The bed sheets are unnaturally neat; they're too even, too still. This place is a mausoleum.

I've been in here only twice before, and I was so little I don't remember anything vividly. When I became a teenager, my parents barred me from entering their room at all. If I needed to see them, they would both come out of the room. This is essentially my first time being inside.

I don't know where to start looking. My parents are skilled enough in their secrecy that it's unlikely they've left behind a dossier revealing everything I want to know. Deep down I know that's what I want to find in this place, but I try my best to keep some sense of realism. If her job is as classified as it is to her own family, she's probably not keeping anything here that would incriminate her. That, of course, drives my curiosity even more. I see a scrapbook on one of the warped wooden bedside tables, and figure that's my mother's side of the bed. I walk over to it and open the top drawer.

There's no dossier. In fact, there's not much of anything. An old tube of chapstick, a pair of nail clippers, and a beat up notepad, but not much else. I reach into the far end of the drawer when I feel something slightly sticky graze my hand. I pull the drawer out to its maximum length and look in when I see it: a strip of duct tape dangles from the underside of the drawer, flimsily hanging on to the top. I realize that it was likely holding something to the top of the drawer.

"What the hell—"

It could have been holding up anything, really, but naturally my mind began computing anything she might keep hidden in her drawer that way: a gun, a storage device of some kind, keys to some secret plane somewhere. Admittedly, all of this was coming from my limited viewing of spy films, but it was better than nothing. Mom sure as hell never gave me any clues.

I go to pull off the tape, but it comes off immediately at my touch. This thing has seen its years. Feeling the sticky side of the tape, I realize it wouldn't hold anything with a decent amount of weight anymore. I run my hand along the top of the drawer to see if there was any unusual shape embossed into the wood. There was nothing there except for a splinter that dug its way into the tip of my middle finger.

"Son of a bitch."

It's one of those thick splinters, the kind that are easy to pull out but hurt like all hell. I yank it out, sending a few drops of blood into the drawer. Though I wipe them up quickly with my shirt-sleeve, smudges of blood can still be seen on the wood. Hoping that Dad never looks into Mom's drawers, I do my best to stick the tape back into the drawer, closing it delicately. There's blood still running down my finger, but I wipe it off with my sleeves every minute or so, hoping that I don't leave any more evidence behind.

Turning around, I see the slide doors to the closet and realize there's got to be something in there that she keeps from work. I open the closet and, much to my happiness, I see stacks upon stacks of cardboard filing boxes.

*Jackpot.*

I see immediately that it'd be damn near impossible for me to remove a box without making it look like someone had been in here. Boxes line the closet from floor to ceiling; I don't know how she managed to fit them all in the first place. Many of the boxes are crinkled or sagging, the weight of all of the other boxes atop them crushing them down. They all bear labels, some with family-sounding names, others with obscure locations. "Vacation '99." "Montenegro." "Christmas 2000." "Lyon." I see one that's looser than most in the stack, labeled "Vienna." I gingerly remove it from the stack, holding the boxes above it so that they don't fall into place loudly.

I go to take the box to the bed, hoping that upon opening it I find at least a modicum of information, but before I make it to the lifeless mattress I feel the lightness of the box. There are maybe one or two things in here.

"Do you need help Mommy?"

She walks quickly down the hall, staring intently at the door to her room. She had been carrying boxes like that into her room all afternoon. Upon hearing my voice, she stops dead in the middle of the hallway.

"What'd you say, honey?" she asks. She hadn't seen me in the doorway to the kitchen.

"Do you need help? You look tired."

She smiles. "Oh, well, that's very kind of you, but I'm fine, you don't need to worry about me. You should go and play with your sister out on the beach, it's nice out today."

"Those look heavy, Mommy. I can help you."

She walks over to me and pats me on the head. "I know you're strong honey, but this is something I have to do by myself. And don't worry, they aren't too heavy. Just some papers and things, that's all."

"What kind of papers?"

Her smile fades a little. She leans over and kisses me on the forehead. Proceeding to walk briskly down the hallway, she says without looking at me, "Go back outside, honey. It's a nice day out."

A couple of manila folders lay gutted at the bottom of the box. The tabs on the folders have been torn off, though some flecks of black ink can be seen on the folder below where the tabs once were. I go back to the closet and take two more boxes, but find nothing more than what was in the first one. Just the boneyard of stories I'll never get to hear. Upon softly knocking on the rest of the boxes in the closet, it becomes plain there's nothing more than the hollow echo that emits from each of them. Why she would choose to keep all of these here if they were empty is beyond me.

Setting the boxes I pulled out back into the closet, my hopes are even lower than when I came into the room. What appeared to be a vault housing my mother's true identity is nothing more than a collection of spent boxes. Their emptiness is matched only by my knowledge of my mother.

Perhaps it was some dark irony, some prank my mother decided to pull on me as the years went on. She knew that I'd never stop asking questions about her job; I never gave up as a teenager, and I sure as hell wasn't going to give up as an adult. Maybe she's not even out on work at all anymore, and she's putting on some elaborate show until I realize that she's never going to tell me any of her secrets. She's spent enough time trying to teach me that; I wouldn't put it beyond her.

Maybe she and Dad have some kind of open marriage, and she's always gone seeing another family all these times Dad's made it seem like she was out working. On my most bitter nights I think to myself that she has another family, one that she betrays as much as she betrays us when she leaves for months or years on end. For all I know she could have some beach house somewhere else, filled with equally false family photographs. There could be a whole other me somewhere in the country, wondering where the hell it is his mother goes all the time. It's darkly consoling in a way, even though I know I don't want it to be true.

Kara is probably going come looking for me any second, giving us just enough time to reconstruct the façade for Mom's arrival. I survey the room one more time, hoping to find some keyhole that leads to a safe where all of her secrets lie. I know it's ludicrous, but it's the only thing I can think of. There's nothing even remotely conspicuous, but upon seeing a desk in the corner of the room I figure that'd be my best shot at finding anything.

The desk is even more weathered than the bedside tables. My parents didn't spend a ton of time in this room, but now it looks like they never left it. The desk feels used, beaten, like it was tired of being in such a dark, vacuous place. There are some neatly piled magazines, the boring *National Geographic*-type stuff my Dad likes, as well as some typical desk items like a pencil holder, but nothing else of note. Of course there's a family picture from when Kara graduated high school—God forbid Mom work here without being reminded of how perfect we are—but surprisingly it's just as worn as the desk is. A film of dust obscures the picture, and the frame is chipped all around the edges. As ugly as it looks, it might be the most honest family picture I've ever seen of us.

I open the top drawer and my heartbeat picks up. There's a big stack of manila folders; they're all inconspicuously labeled, but at least it's something. The top one reads "TAXES."


"What do you mean, we don't have to pay taxes on the beach house?" Dad asks.

"You see now why I've always been the one to do the taxes? That's a loophole that I've specifically arranged for us. They told me—"

"You didn't think that I would have to do the taxes eventually? You're gone a lot of the time—"

"I know that," Mom snaps. "Do you think I don't know that?"

"No, that's not what I said, I just meant that I didn't know how you wanted to do the taxes if you weren't here when we get them in the mail."

I came into the kitchen for a glass of water, but upon hearing my parents' raised voices I know I have a chance at finally hearing something. I stood with my back against the wall next to the door of the living room, right across from the entry to the kitchen. I was supposed to be asleep two hours ago.

"Look, obviously I can't give too much away, but I've declared the beach house something of an asset. You know, because of the... the things I keep stored there."

"Uh-huh. Is it... okay? I mean, is it legal?"

She pauses for a moment. "Technically, no, but... because of the position I'm in, I have a little more... leniency, I'd say. I'm not going rogue or anything, I have approval to do this."

"Is that how we got the price we did on the house?"

"No, that was sheer luck. I got the approval to do this two years after we bought the place."

"So... do you want me to do it still? I can do it, it's just, you'll have to show me how."

Mom sighs. "Don't worry about it tonight, I'll show you tomorrow while the kids are at school. I'll call in and let them know I'll be late."

"Okay."

"I'm sorry, I didn't mean to make you feel excluded—"

"It's fine," Dad says. "Don't worry about it, I'm not mad, it just confused me, is all. And, in any case, it saves us a nice chunk of money."

I hear them kiss. I lean in closer to hear more, but as I do, the sound of footsteps on the wooden floor come closer and closer. Quickly, I run into the kitchen and hide behind the central island. The footsteps stop in front of the door to the kitchen; my heart beats rapidly. Moments pass like hours until finally the footsteps continue their way down the hall.

The folder contains old tax documents, nothing revealing. But as I remember that conversation all those years ago, the post-it note atop one of the documents makes a lot more sense:

> Harriet,
> Don't worry, the new guy knows about your situation with the beach house. File it as you always do, and there won't be any problems. Good of you to check though.
> -P.

The note looks old; it's attached to a document dated five years ago. I look through some of the signatures and names, finding no one with a "P" as an initial. *Figures.*

Unsurprisingly, the rest of the desk drawers are filled with documents that reveal nothing of import. All of this tax information is pretty harmless; there's no reason they should have to hide it from me. Neither of them ever figured out that I had eavesdropped on the conversation back then, so they were likely under the impression that I knew nothing about this house's tax status. But whatever it was my mother kept here that allowed her a tax-exempt status on the house seemed to have disappeared. There are no mysterious pieces of duct tape in these drawers, only meaningless documents and office supplies. But just before I begin to leave the room, I notice something beneath the stack of magazines. Lifting the stack up, I take the envelope smashed underneath it.

The first things that catch my eye are the stamps. There are several of them, all of them foreign—I can't peg where from. There is no return address, and our address is written in handwriting so sloppy I'm surprised the mail service could have deciphered it. Looking anxiously at the door, I remove the letter from the envelope.

"Dad, don't you ever get tired of waiting for Mom to come home?"

Dad looks up from his newspaper. "What do you mean?"

I struggle to find the words. "I mean, I'm happy when she comes home and everything, but I just get tired of all of the waiting. It shouldn't have to be an event for me to see my mom. I should be able to see her without having to count down the precious minutes until she's gone again."

Dad sets the newspaper on the coffee table and folds his arms. "Are you not happy your mother is actually going to be here for your graduation?"

"I am, but—"

"And haven't you learned by now that your mother makes immense sacrifices for this family?"

"I know—"

"Really? You do? Because from all the moping you do, it sure doesn't seem like it."

"Is this not hard on you, Dad? I mean, really, are you just so used to this that it's natural to hardly be around the woman you love?"

He gets up from his chair and brushes off the crumbs of the coffee cake he made for Mom's return. He comes over to the couch and sits down next to me. I scoot away to give us space, but he moves in closer, staring sternly at me.

"It's hard every day she's not here. Don't get it in your head that it's ever easy. It's painful. It hurts. But I love your mother, and as a result I respect the choices she's made for her life. I know it's hard on you—"

"No, you don't know. At least you get to know what she's doing."

"I don't get to know everything."

"But you get to know something!" I jump up from the couch. "Don't think I haven't heard those conversations in the living room all of these years. Yeah, she may have never formally 'briefed' you, but it's tons more than what I get to know. I get to know her job is difficult and, of course, classified. Apparently, you're trustworthy, but I'm not. Because I'm just a stupid kid."

Dad remains on the couch for a few moments. "Son," he says, getting up off the couch, "There will come a day where your mother will come home for the last time. She'll come home and she'll be here. I don't know when that day is, and I'm pretty sure she doesn't either. But for now, we just have to grit our teeth and keep on living. Your sister and I have learned that lesson, and it's high time you did as well."

Behind me, I can hear the click-clack of my mom's heels coming up the walkway.

"Fine."

The letter is written in an anonymous typewriter font, dated to a week and a half ago.

> *Derrick,*
> *This letter violates all of the rules about these sorts of things, but Harriet's too important for you to not be told this.*
>
> *What's been happening over here has been danger-ous, more dangerous than anything we've ever done.*
>
> *One night, things went bad. Lies were told, people were double-crossed—and in the mix of that situ-ation, Harriet was killed. It wasn't because of any lack in her or us; the circumstances changed radi-cally, and she happened to catch the worst of it.*

*Protocol says that we aren't supposed to tell you this until a representative can come speak to you, but because of Harriet's significance I felt you deserved to hear it from one of us. She wasn't just collateral damage; she was one of us, probably even the best of us.*

*No one else knows that I sent this letter, so please destroy after reading.*

Outside, I hear the sound of a car pulling up into the driveway. Doors open, and the sound of boots stomping on our pebble walkway gets closer and closer.

From the kitchen, I hear, "Gramma's here! Gramma's here!"

"Kara, go see if that's my *belle de jour.* I think it is!"

# THE TRAGEDY

## EMILY AUMAN

I want to be Holly Golightly," she told me as she held a glass of bourbon on the rocks. She had long, dark hair and a voice smooth as silk.

"Audrey Hepburn is very beautiful." I said. I kept messing with the watch that wrapped around my left wrist; it was new and didn't feel quite right yet.

"No," she corrected, taking a large gulp, "I don't want to be Audrey Hepburn. Have you seen Roman Holiday?" she glanced up at me and scoffed, "Who would want to be that simple and naïve? I don't want to be Audrey Hepburn. I want to be Holly Golightly."

"Why?" I asked, still observing the newness of my watch. The girl was pretty, sure, even beautiful. Either way, I had more important things on my mind, like finding a slightly less glamorous woman to fill the void I suffered. Or for me to fill her void, if we're being honest.

"I want to be frightening but charming, gorgeous but honest, passionate but apathetic." Her long lashes lined sparkling green eyes.

"Well, you need an orange tabby." After this bit of information, I was spent of any memories from the movie.

"I already have one," she smiled slyly, "an orange tabby that's kind of fat; he's nameless." She smiled more, to herself this time. She wore obnoxiously high heels that she hooked on the bar-stool's base, the spikes accented long, soft legs.

"Perfect," I remarked.

"What character are you?" she asked me tenderly.

"I'm sorry?"

"Breakfast at Tiffany's, who are you?"

"I'm afraid I've only seen it once." She was really starting to bore me; the girl clearly had no other interests. Her cry for at-tention was too desperate for my taste.

"That's terrible!" She gasped and took another drink, taking a moment to gain composure. "I think you're Paul. You're defi-nitely Paul." I shrugged. This meant nothing to me and she meant nothing to me. I turned my body away from her, trying to show I didn't care what she had to say. She tapped me on the shoulder.

"What is it?" I said.

"Would you mind?" She asked, leadingly.

"Would I mind what?"

"You see that guy over there?" she pointed to a man wearing a suit sitting in a particularly dark corner with a much younger woman on his lap.

"Yes. What about him?"

"That's an ex-lover of mine." I wasn't even slightly surprised.

"Okay, what do you want me to do about it? I'm not going to fight him or anything."

"Oh, heavens no!" she put her hand on my tricep and I looked at it, I'm not a huge fan of affection. "I want you to escort me home, please."

I thought of every possible solution, trying to conjure a way I could politely say no. I quickly realized such a solution didn't exist. My parents had raised me in the South and I knew there was no excuse to let a woman walk home alone at night.

"Alright, come on." I laid a twenty on the table and nodded to the new bartender. Back in the good days I would've taken the former bartender, Michelle, home. But she left town and I'd been lonelier ever since. The new bar girl wasn't my style; her eyes and skin were too light. She looked like every other girl, not exotic enough.

"Isn't it a beautiful night?" Holly Golightly asked me as we walked outside. It wasn't great out. Kind of cloudy and very cold. Not my favorite weather.

"It's alright."

"What's your name, anyway?"

"Joshua."

"Okay, Josh."

"No," I corrected this time, "not Josh, Joshua. What's your name?"

"Grace."

"Really? You don't hear that name much."

"Yes," She straightened her neck, becoming taller in a sort of defense. "My mother was obsessed with Grace Kelly, so she named me Grace."

"Interesting."

"Whenever I heard news reporters mention 'Princess Grace' growing up, I always thought it was me. My father always said they were talking about me. He'd sit me in his lap while my mother cooked dinner and he'd say 'Little Gracie, you're the real Princess Grace'. I was eleven before I realized I wasn't actually a princess." I rolled my eyes to myself. "That was a sad day. Oh, we have to go left here." We walked down a well-lit street, the middle-to-upper class homes stacked in suburban rows.

"So what's your middle name?"

"Kelly."

"Wow."

"Yes. I've met someone named Danielle Steel though, so I think I did fairly well. I'm right here." She pulled me along to the basement door of a two-story colonial home, fumbling with keys until she stuck the right one in. "It isn't much," she prefaced, "but it keeps me dry and fabulous." She smiled wobbly, crooked and lazy from the alcohol.

I was appalled. The inside looked like a bunker, no kind of paneling or wallpaper or paint. Plain sheetrock. In the middle of the front room was an old orange couch, falling apart and stained. Across from it, against the wall, was an old television with a VCR built-in. She flung her shoes off and landed on the pitiful couch.

"Would you be a dear and put in the movie?"

"What movie?" I was stupid enough to ask.

"The only movie I have, darling, 'Breakfast at Tiffany's.' Just hit play on the television." I obeyed and the opening credits began to roll.

"I'd best be going." I stared uncomfortably at the dirty walls that enclosed the stunning girl.

"Oh alright, well, please leave your address and I'll make sure you receive something for your kindness."

"That's really unnecessary, Grace."

"I insist," she said firmly from the corner of her mouth, her eyes were glued to the screen as Audrey Hepburn stepped out of a taxi cab.

"Well okay." I succumbed and left my address on a scrap of paper I found on a foldable card table set up to resemble something like a desk. I never expected to hear from Grace again and I can't say I thought I was going to miss her.

Two days later I saw her again, in black and white. "Young Woman Commits Suicide" the newspaper read blankly. I was standing inside a convenience store, preparing to buy my usual Newports and grape Fanta. Her picture looked at me in a way that was sad and pitiful. If someone ends their life the day after they've met you, you can't help but feel guilty. I picked up the paper and kept reading.

"Grace Mosteller, 24, was found in her small basement apartment late yesterday." I read on, and shuddered, "The woman was found with dull razors embedded along the entirety of her legs and arms; her feet, breasts and hands had suffered third degree burns and ,according to the police, she died of pesticide poisoning. 'Evidently the girl wanted to die,' said Officer Hastings, 'and she wanted to die gruesomely. Dramatically. Our hearts go out to those who knew this confused young woman.'" I stopped reading. I never thought Grace would've killed herself.

I had finally pushed Grace out of my mind again when, the next day, something came in the mail.

"Dear Paul,

Your kindness is refreshing. Keep being so wonderful, dear?

Yours, Grace."

Should I have stayed with her that night and watched Breakfast at Tiffany's? Should I have cared at all? I immediately went to the movie store and walked to the 'B's.

"Is there something we can help you with, sir?"

an overweight woman with short blonde curls approached.

"Breakfast at Tiffany's."

"Breakfast at Tiffany's, sir?"

"Yes," I snapped at her and she startled. "Breakfast at Tiffany's!" She rushed over and ran her pale, chubby fingers through the movies. Expertly she searched and I fumed behind her. I wasn't mad at her. Or at anyone. Except maybe the director of this god-forsaken film. Finally the blonde woman handed the movie back to me.

"Did you know this is based on a book?" she said as she rang it up on the register just a moment later.

"No, no I didn't."

"Most people don't." she said, prideful of her own knowledge. I wonder if Grace had known. I wonder if Grace had ever read it.

This is my older brother's story. This is how he told it, making it sound like he was some sort of mysterious, James Dean character. He repeated the story many times over before he died. Of course, he died not long after Grace Mosteller committed suicide, he died of loneliness. He would've said he died of heartbreak, he was one for romances. In fact, he claimed he loved Grace Mosteller even though all he knew was that she loved Holly Golightly and her mother loved Grace Kelly. He said that was reason enough, the crazy bastard. He stopped going to work; he just watched that stupid movie over and over. There was nothing I could do. I found him on his bed; he looked peaceful, asleep. The way people should look when they're found dead, I guess. To be honest it's the most relaxed I'd ever seen him and between you and me, his death was a relief. He was never happy. He did it with extra strength Tylenol and a bottle of Jack Daniels, like a true coward. His last words were written on a piece of paper, on his nightstand:

> "I'm like cat here, a no-name slob. We belong to nobody, and nobody belongs to us. We don't even belong to each other."

# SHARDS: CO-OPTING STS

## ST STRELITZ

A mermaid curled up
reading HER, book,
beside the brook
with flowing locks
of ebony hair, each one
swirling and twirling
in the wind:
Clutching out toward some definition of herself,
she found that 'I am Her Gart' didn't let her hold on...
She was not Gart, she was not Hermione,
she was not any more Her Gart, what was she?[1]

*Hermione. Her-my-one. Her explores the relationship between the self and the essence of one's self—the relationship between "Her," "I," and "she" all under one umbrella, Hermione. She suffers from an odd brand of dementia, but still, "Her represents an inquiry into the workings of identity."[2]*

# SUMMER

"Ani rotzah t'marim, ach'shav" (*reish* pronounced like the *erre*); her laughter like clucking bouncing off the hashish haze, ricocheting off the tapestry-covered walls. Thinking about the pyramids of dates on that truck that gave her a lift 3 hours ago, she drooled slightly. Thirst abated by a Parliament Light. "Sasha'ed be pissed. Fuck Sasha, fatass—" the Galgalatz DJ announced MJ. In a whirl, she got up, cig in mouth, body sticky from stagnant sweat; steaming swivels of incense interrupted by her movement. *Wanna be startin' somethin'*—everything rhythmically swayed with her; the room seemed to dance with the bomb shelter under it. Exchanging cig for j, one more toke— GHB flashback—glimmer subsided, eyes dulled, depression juices surged; all because of that almost-faded hickey.

Crinkle. Rip. Crush. Grind. Place. Roll. Smoke.

Empty, devoid of trustworthiness, LOST , she watched Tabula Rasa for the third time: "Iteration #..." She thought ahead to the Walkabout, to the White Rabbit, to Humpty Dumpty. Then, no beamish boy, she chortled and burbled: "it's brillig and twenty, time to gyre a j"[3]

Crinkle. Rip. Crush. Grind. Place. Roll. Smoke.

"One two! One two! And through and through,"[4] pregger-pause, "what's vorpal? Hmmm..."

# AUTUMN

November 17, 1998

Rewind: November 17, 1986 was a full moon (Mami claims a blue moon, but my AOL search claims otherwise). Hollywood, Florida is clustered with all kinds of folks who welcome Sasha into the world. At Memorial, Gila-monster is tipsy off Grey

Goose, "What's a Sasha?" she giggles. Brian beamed, "my beautiful little girl." Giggles, "she's hairy!" Nono and Nona jeer from the corner.

<u>Today, my 12th birthday</u>: It's not a full moon, and my Pocahontas hair is kinking up all Jew-like (likely because I've been bleeding for about 2 years. Thinking about Russian Sasha and Greek Alexander, I sort through my gifts—birthday, surgery, birthday, Hanukkah, surgery, birthday, Hanukkah—and think about how my boy name means "man's protector." But, anyone who is alive and speaks Swahili knows about the Sasha spirits: present time, recent past, near future, just not limitless past. Sasha time actually exists (so do I have to worry about always being late? ☺), but it's not like a Zamani sea-sponge that absorbs every experience e v e r. It'd be so cool if I fell in love with some regal Ethiopian or some dreadlock Rasta named Zamani.

(The doodle below is of our wedding-invite: an ocean of time depicting our reality – neither after nor before; Sasha and Zamani, Zamani and Sasha.[5])

17 days till I'm fastened with Harrington rods.

Happy birthday, Sasha Tamar Strelitz.

<3 <3 <3

STS

# WINTER

*I. Downt her abbith ole*
One pill makes you larger
And one pill makes you small
And the ones that mother gives you
Don't do anything at all.
Go ask Alice[6] about this cocktail:

2 kadurim – Diclofenac

1 kadur – Percocet

3 kadurim – Baclofen

1.5 grams of ganja

babe my sweet ganja babe

I love the way ya love me and the way ya misbehavin'

ganja babe my sweet ganja babe[7]

is the epitome of a green TA

(let 'em think that means eco-friendly).


Lacan says infants view the border between

internal and external

worlds fluidly as one.[8]

Mirror-Stage ➜ the "psychoanalytic experience"

when the "I" is revealed.[9]

Signifier/signified help categorize

images and feelings

(later associated with words).[10]

First Encounter (1997) with subjectivity—

ego

forms, formulates.[11]

Autonomousness.


Sister morphine when you *aint* comin' round again.[12]

Booyah achieved!

*II. Gematria: HER*

is an artist, dreamer, stargazer,

Bohemian&rebel with rings on her fingers

and bells on her shoes
(and I knew without askin' she was into the blues).[13]
Live in the now!
(aka New-Agey bullshit.)
Tattoos are for goyim, but patchouli is for
hippie-dippies, and Virginia is for
loverrrs.
All 20 nails groomed (mighty well),
Her incessantly burns incense
and diffuses oils. Wicked insomnia
(an' 18,000 attempts at meditation).
The Big O Moment spray-painted
in pink and purple dressed in
black.
(Sincere attempt to incorporate more color.)
Soft skin n' cute smile
(like Sarah Silverman or Nancy Botwin).
Signing off.
P.s. Look at those mascaraed eyes
fluttering to the
beat beat beat
of their own drum
(drum drum...
OCD).
P.p.s. 200 40 400 5 300 60
!!!!!!!5 40 6 60 100 1 10 5
III. "F" is for Fuck
As he silently guzzles Duff,
She fervently tickles her muff.

No. Not. Ever. Enough.

Too much puff-puff,

too strong this stuff!

It makes coming tough.

Ugh...Anyway,

Goooooooooooo Buffs!

*IV. My Sprechgesang*

She Belongs To Me (Dylan @ Cruzan, June, 2013),

and youngin' After the Goldrush.

    Spirit animal: Janis Joplin.

    Cat's name: Stevie Nicks.

History, language, sex (interest piqued);

also, the (dis)similarities betwixt

people and cultures.

She paints her daytime black;[14]

and cooks some stellar dishes (dy-na-mite).

She emphasizing her right brain, but

excells in math (maths?).

Scorpius signifies: sexual, strong-willed,

sensitive, salacious, secretive, shrewd...

Born a bubbe!

My beauty like her's.

Groooovy groovin'

on a Sunday afternoon—

HIP-HUG HER![15]

*V. The Count counts*

cinco,

five,

chamesh.

VI. Transcending that æolian harp (alo: fragmented, dreamy visions)

.§†§. I don't look back through the mothers, but through the visionary (Indian) angels. Like, Willie W. who poeticized David's strumming, cause it's the wind! ("It's a car that runs on water, man!")[16] Or, Sammy-Sam's pleasure-dome peppered with caves of ice—Xaaanaduuuuuuu![17] Frankenstein's bolts screamed Figment's *imaaaaginaaation*.

.§†§. A wee bit later and across t h e Pond, good ole Ralphie pondered the Poet and the Over-Soul. His thoughts in Circles whilst his beau, Henry-D shacked up in some wooden shack (all for you, nature, (the) yada yada yada). And because grassy leaves pissed off ole Ralphie, Henry-D didn't get his dick sucked for 2 years (and change).

.§†§. Walt (not the little black boy from LOST Walt, but the bearded, white, everyman, lover of all, cooky-genius Walt) cross'd in that Brooklyn Ferry to go visit Miss–Em–D. Like a frog on a lily pad, she felt that formal feeling; but she didn't stop for no death! And hell if she kept the bloody Sabbath in church! She threw bobolinks at him, and he still loved her (and the bobolinks). And then, they both got drunk on that sweet nectar we call success.

.§†§. After 40-some magical years, tadaaa! Ali Ginsy (not Ali Baba) howled and howled, waving genitals and manuscripts, and genitals.[18] Expulsion from Columbia was

e x p l o s i v e !!! POP! BANG! Dharma bumming and peyote and Moloch and poeticized lion-roaring and daddy-o and benzadrine and Buddhism and gay sex and straight sex and sex, sex, sex.

.§†§. So, why don't we do it in the road[19] like Snoopy and Woodstock?

.§†§. Then, the hipster ruined it for all of us.

VII. *7 for all mankind*

Do: Creation/Shabbat. Re: Golden menorah (well, any menorah). Mi: Egyptian famine. Fa: Jericho. So: Solomon's Temple.
La: Joseph's cows. Ti: Tefilin. 735.

# Spring

Dreading Summer. All I can think about is upcoming Summer.
Humidity forms beads of sweat on my upper lip reminding me
Summer is coming. *The Bell Jar* took place in the Summer. The
humidity entraps me in a bell jar. Ever since the GHB...Fuck-
ing Summer. Medicine holidays all in the Summer. The bubble
always bursts in the Summer. (Where in the world is Summer
Sanders?) Always in the Summer.

---

[1] Doolittle, Hilda. HERmione. New York: New Directions,
1981. Web. 1 July 2013.

[2] Galtung, Ingrid. "Becoming HERmione: An Exploration
of the Process of Subjectivity in H.D.'s HER." University
of Bergen (2010): 12. Web. 1 July 2013.

[3] Carroll, Lewis. The Looking-Glass and What Alice Found
There. New York: Rand, McNally, & Co., 1917. Web. 2
July 2013.

[4] Carroll, Lewis.

[5] Mbiti, John S. African Religions and Philosophy. 2nd ed.
Oxford: Heinemann Educational Publishers, 1969. Web.
2 July 2013.

[6] Jefferson Airplane. "White Rabbit." Surrealistic Pillow.
RCA Victor, 1967. MP3.

[7] Michael Franti and Spearhead. "Ganja Babe." Weeds: Music From the Original Series. 2005. MP3.

[8] Thompson, Theresa. "Jacques Lacan: 'Mirror Stage' and
'Instance of the Letter.'" Valdosta State University. 23 Feb-

ruary 2011. Web. 1 July 2013. Lecture slides.

9 Lacan, Jacques. The Seminar of Jacques Lacan: The Psychoses (Book III). Ed. Jacques-Alain Miller. Trans. Russell Grigg. New York: W. W. Norton & Company, 1993. Web. 1 July 2013.

10 Lacan, Jacques.

11 Lacan, Jacques.

12 Rolling Stones. "Sister Morphine." Sticky Fingers. Olympic Studios, 1971. MP3.

13 Grateful Dead. "Scarlet Begonia." Grateful Dead from the Mars Hotel. Grateful Dead, 1974. MP3.

14 Dylan, Bob. "She Belongs to Me." Bringing it All Back Home. Columbia, 1965. Compact disc.

15 The Rascals. "Groovin." Hip-Hug Her. Stax Records, 1967. MP3.

16 "Pilot." That '70s Show. Fox. 23 Aug 1998. Television.

17 Coleridge, Samuel. "Kubla Khan." Poetry Foundation. N.d. Web. 3 July 2013.

18 Ginsberg, Allen. Howl and Other Poems. San Francisco: City Lights Books, 1956. Web. 17 Nov 2012.

19 Beatles. "Why Don't We Do It in the Road?" The Beatles. Apple Records, 1968. MP3.

# THE UNORTHODOX & ECCENTRIC DETOUR OF THE TEENAGE DREAM

## SPIDER MCQUEEN

I almost believed I would spend the rest of my life sleeping on floors. The unconventional comfort of sleeping on a pallet of winter coats covered in thrift store quilts in the back of a van had been with me for as long as I can remember. It just didn't seem suitable to be forced to sleep on a wiry mattress... in a strange house no less. It was already too quiet at night to sleep. When I finally slipped into a light snooze just as the sun was peeking through the curtains, I woke up with the taste of fresh urine on my lips, a prank from one of the three hideous boys I was forced to live with. He managed to sneak into my room during my forced unconsciousness. I grudgingly spent my teenage years with pent-up frustration, worry and rage living as a foster child after they arrested my father and towed our van away. In my fourteenth year, I was a volcano waiting to spit fire; burning a vicious house that would never be my home. That was the year my tumultuous eruption would make its appearance in the record books of Child Protective Services.

I spent the remainder of my last middle school year and the beginning of my high school freshman life walking back from a strange school, to an even stranger house belonging to two of the most apathetic and neglectful foster parents a lonely girl could ever cry herself to sleep over. To make matters worse, I was unfortunate to be the only sane person under a roof full of derelict future criminals. I always had to be on defense; my nerves ravaged and paranoid from stupid pranks that went uncontrolled. I secretly slept with a small fire extinguisher near my pillow. It was to replace the pepper spray I bought from a boy at school during detention, but was soon confiscated by the foster adults. It would be too late by time they realized it was a matter of survival due to their blatant refusal to take control of the situation. I took my self-defense seriously. I *was* the only teenage girl after all.

The boys I lived with were simply wretched. I was slowly blossoming into a young woman while idling by in a puddle of social backwash; clearly better off living with my father in our van than dealing with what that old bag of a bitch from social services brought me to. If only I had a shovel and a bag of lime the day that stone-faced woman took me away; I already had my eye on a plot of land I planned on making nice and fertile with her remains. Hell, I might have even planted some wildflowers to beautify the turned ground and mask the stink of her rotting flesh. Unfortunately, unless you're a cop, murder is illegal.

Luckily, I didn't have to share a room with anyone in that terrible, emotionless house. That was looking at the glass half-full. There was no lock on the door, unfortunately, so I had to slide the heavy bedroom armoire in front of my door every night and move it every morning when it was time to leave for school. That worked only for a few days until the foster lady of the house, Miss Lorraine, demanded I move it. It was replaced by two nightstands the next day when I returned from school, much to my dismay. The armoire didn't stop those horrible little savages from coming in through the window to spray me with a skunk they found in the woods. I took up girls' softball just so my foster parents would let me keep a baseball bat in my room. My excitement grew like a weed for the precious day I could whip my bat out from underneath my bed and clock a canyon in their worthless skulls; all of them! I daydreamed about my fingers vibrating under the weight of my swing, that glorious metal bat touching bone and obliterating the structure of their heads. I daydreamed until goose bumps sprouted up along the flesh of my arms and down my spine and into my girly parts. I wouldn't stop until everyone's head looked like plum pudding against their precious, cotton pillowcases; and only then would I rob them blind. I would catch a train all the way to Mexico and wait there quietly until my father got out of prison. It was one of the many diabolical plans I acted out in my head at night as I lay in a heap of blankets on the floor at the foot of my bed. Escape was a primal instinct lying inside the ulcer of rage in my belly. I would do anything to leave; I kept a small suitcase with two changes of clothes and some bare essentials under my bed. When that magical time finally arrived, I would leave and never look back.

The three boys were taken from their home just like I was. They were half-brothers with different fathers; ages spanning from eleven years old to fifteen. I didn't know what happened to their fathers, but I did know their mother was going to prison, I heard them talking in the backyard when my window wasn't entirely shut. Their mother used to cook up crack cocaine in their kitchen when she thought they were asleep. It was a shame she had more time to cook up drugs than whip her kid's asses like they obviously needed. She should have known it was long overdue. It was indeed a shame from an outside perspective, but the boys still had each other; I didn't have anyone.

Lorraine and her husband Andrew were the appointed foster parents of us kids. They were in their late 40's and flabby as hell. They were the epitome of what would happen to a couple who ate fast food every single night for all eternity. They reminded me of the Michelin man; they both had boobs running along the top of their stomachs like two sandwich bags half-filled with school-grade glue. They were two horrible human science experiments gone awry and I prayed one day I would find them in front of the television; their arm flab slumped over their La-Z-Boy's, morsels of McSausage-biscuit lodged down their swollen windpipes. I imagined I would snatch their wallets and live off their credit cards until I could find a decent job in Mexico. Andrew and Lorraine were clearly unconcerned about minding a bunch of rowdy boys. It was easy to see by their actions (or lack thereof) they were too busy deciding what toppings they wanted on their pizza to mind their household, while their large government checks financed their raging gluttony. I suppose all the mindless eating and sleeping distracted them, and I suffered for it. I knew something had to be done once and for all.

Nobody could take the place of my father. I was a Daddy's girl. It wasn't long after he first pressed a wine cooler to my lips at the age of three that we became the best drinking buddies a father and a daughter could ever be. I remember it was bubbly and delicious. Soda was soon replaced by wine coolers at my request. I was okay with my father's alcohol problem, especially after I got drunk. His excessive drinking kept him from holding a job, and after a while it became easier for us to just live out of his old conversion van on the tiny monthly check he received from his stint in the Navy. Perhaps his habits swayed a bit out of control, but who could blame the guy? My mother had decided one day to leave the house for cigarettes and never came back. I believe he did the best he could with what he had, and the knowledge that was given to him. When the truancy officers were notified of my excessive absences and the Child protective Services were looking for him, he knew it was all over. He stopped taking me to school and we lived in Walmart parking lots for two years until they caught him with his pants down, literally. He was found by a paranoid farmer's wife as he lay recovering from a black-out in a cow pasture a little over a mile from where the van was parked. The cops took him in and booked him for several warrants out for his arrest. He was too hung over to realize what was happening until it was too late. Several hours later, the police woke me from my comfortable vehicular slumber with such horrific banging on the windshield, I thought I was parked near a construction site. They found me, a twelve year old, unwashed little girl sleeping in the back of a van littered with empty beer cans, an ashtray full of cigarette butts and too many partially-smoked joints. I haven't seen him since.

He was a lonely man and needed a friend more than a daughter at that time in his life. I loved him; still do. After Mom left, he didn't date anyone else. I truly hoped he didn't do anything stupid after going to prison. He was never the sharpest hook in the tackle box. I haven't heard from him in months. I pray every night to an unknown god that he knows where I am or at least knows I'm alright. He's all I know.

I was four years old when my mother left, so when my father was taken from me and I realized I was all alone, I cried for breakfast, lunch and dinner for weeks. I lost quite a lot of weight and was labeled an anorexic. My file declared I had an eating disorder due to my father's abuse: so far from the truth, horrific lies to make it that much harder for my father to get me back. If by some chance I looked out the window and saw my father's sloppy grin smiling back at me from Miss Lorraine's driveway, I would piss my pants. I would give anything to see my Dad again... even my life.

It was a rainy morning when I decided that I wouldn't be coming back after school. I was late for school almost every morning, waiting at my bedroom window, staring at the empty driveway before Miss Lorraine got angry and threatened to send me to a group home. She told me she would make sure my father would never be able to find me if I kept up my bad behavior. That day I left extra early so I wouldn't have to hear her goddamn mouth when I slipped past her open bedroom door. I knew I would have to return for money, but I had bigger fish to fry. During the middle of the night, while everyone slept, I pulled apart the plastic capsules of an entire bottle of sleeping pills, purchased from the same boy I met in detention, and drugged all the beverages in the refrigerator. I'm pretty sure I seriously overdid it. Before long, the adults would drink their morning milk, juice or whatever other viciously tainted beverage waited for them in the refrigerator. I would wait safely at school until the lunch bell rang, then sneak out to grab their wallets and car keys without any fuss or fighting.

School was dirty and redundant, like everything else in my life, but my heart raced with anticipation. I practically stared a hole into the clock above the blackboard, waiting for the lunch bell to ring. I was a short, flat-chested girl with no friends; nobody really paid me any attention... a very good thing for me that day. Even the nerds ignored me. After what seemed like an eternity, the bell rang for lunch and I immediately slipped under the long table, while everyone else filed out of the classroom on their way to soggy PB&J's and prison-grade milk. Finally, I heard the tumblers inside the lock indicating that the classroom was secure for the duration of lunch.

The flat-tip screwdriver I packed the night before was all I needed to jimmy open the thickly-paned window behind the teacher's desk. I threw my book bag over the sill and effortlessly hopped over after it without bothering to close anything behind me. It would be the last time I set foot in that school anyways and I sincerely didn't give a shit regardless. As I walked casually back to the foster house, several blocks away in the rain, I managed to crack a smile for the first time since I left my daddy's van.

I arrived at the old, yellowing two story house completely drenched, but giddy with anticipation. The station wagon, unsurprisingly, was still parked in the driveway, just like it was that morning. I went around back to the tree the boys climbed to reach my bedroom window. I quietly landed on my bed inside, and set my book bag on the floor. It was quiet except for the soft patter of rain, and the dull sound of a television left on in another room. I went to the closet to change into dry clothes. When I opened the closet door, I gasped so loud I was sure someone had heard. The oldest boy, J.D., was asleep in my closet between my winter coats, apparently prepared to wait as long as it took to scare the living shit out of me when I returned home from school at the regular time.

"What the fuck are YOU doing here, Asshole?" I whispered. He had his eyes closed and didn't move a muscle, his head was low, his chin resting on his chest.

I kneeled down and lightly blew in his face, causing his boy-bangs to flutter.

No response.

He must've had something to drink that morning; a flowing string of saliva hung out of his open mouth, connecting to the crotch of his jeans as he slumped over cross-legged in my closet. My heart still racing, I quietly changed into dry clothes, careful not to wake him. I had no time for foolish games. I hoped he had enough for a three day coma, more if I was lucky. The duct tape from the kitchen would contain my ignorant intruder should he wake up with a design to ruin my plans.

Clothed and dry again, I checked the house to see if everyone was just as asleep as J.D. I needed to grab all the money I could find and be damned-near out of the state before anyone woke up. I kept my shoes off and only wore socks to be as quiet as possible for my trek to the kitchen. I could hear the faint sound of the television in Miss Lorraine and Andrew's bedroom down the hall.

I knew I had to walk past their room before going in to the kitchen, so I sat at the door of my room for a long period of time, waiting for a rustle or a cough; anything that gave me an indication someone was conscious in the house.

Other than the canned sounds of the blaring television, nothing else seemed to stir. I was able to ninja-like bypass the creaking floorboards and arrive at the door of Miss Lorraine's room. The door opened up to the bed, giving me the sight of one set of feet at the end of it. I popped my head inside to see Andrew silently sleeping with his glasses still on his face. I sighed with relief. He must've had a lot to drink while I was at school. The television sat on a TV tray facing me. I watched the Flintstones for a few seconds. I never was able to watch television while living in the van, and I might have stood there longer than I'd like to admit. When I turned toward the kitchen, I saw Miss Lorraine, in her nightgown, staring dead into my face from across the hall.

She and I were silent for what seemed like forever. The sounds of Fred Flintstone laughing his signature laugh, the only sound be-tween us. She was at one end of the hall while I was at the other. My mind raced over the options I had considered thousands of times during my early morning brainstorms. She was blocking the kitchen from both sides due to her hefty girth. She was holding a cup of coffee, which she drank black. A fact I overlooked when poisoning the household drinks.

Wonderful, maybe I should have gotten to know her better...

"Young lady," Her tone was low and unstable, like a volcano about to erupt, "What...in the Devil's name are you doing here?"

I said nothing, just stared back at her, cursing the creation of coffee. Foul smelling, poor excuse for a drug. I could feel the adrenaline shooting through my body, speeding up my heart rate. My hands were shaking so much I knew she could see it no matter how much I attempted to hide my reaction.

"Answer me, young lady..." she demanded, a rolling boil in her voice.

"JD got me pregnant. He's in my room right now... hiding in my closet." That was not something I had considered when playing this scenario out in my head. I guess some things are better unrehearsed.

We were both silent with surprise, my words hung in the air like a nasty fart. Her eyes grew as large as Easter eggs, her creamy skin flushed into a dark maroon color as she stormed past me down the hall and into my room. I ran past her as I heard the closet door fling open and the gasp of her already labored breath at the sight she saw.

I was already in the kitchen rummaging through the cabinets when she called out for Andrew. Obviously he wasn't answering.

"JD isn't breathing!" was the last thing I heard out of poor Miss Lorraine. She set foot inside the hallway, presumably heading to her unconscious husband. I caught her by complete surprise, knocking her out cold with a cast iron skillet to the forehead. Her skull made the sound of a bell in a church tower. She rolled her eyes up inside her head and fell back into the room like a timbered oak tree. Her body hit the hard wood floor with such force, the entire house shook.

I stood there for a moment; the skillet vibrating like a tuning fork in my shaking hand. I stood above her, marveling at how surreal my day had become.

No time to wonder if she was dead or not. I had to find the keys, the cash and the highway out of town.

I shook myself and grabbed the car keys and both of their wallets. The suitcase I kept under the bed was waiting for me. I slipped on my shoes and marched out of the house; casually locking the door behind me.

I never stopped smiling.

# JP

## DONALD GEORGE LOSEY

Lex and Timmy were seated in the middle of the resort lodge's cavernous, empty, dining hall. They both had half-finished lunches before them, though their attention was focused entirely on the green and black park radio sitting equidistant between them on the polished table top.

"... keep telling you, the Rex isn't our main problem," Dr. Alan Grant stressed, "the Raptors are too damn smart."

"Well, it's all a moot point," John Hammond soothed. Timmy and Lex both adored their grandfather, though Timmy had developed a nerd crush on Grant and was secretly more inclined to agree with him. "The fences will be up soon," he continued. Lex seemed to brighten at his optimism.

"He's right, the Raptors are all really dumb anyway," said an unfamiliar third voice.

"The hell they are!" Muldoon drunkenly yelled, there was the sound of a brief scuffle then Grant was back on, "listen John, the fences aren't enough against the Raps."

"Don't listen to me I'm high on drugs," the third voice cut in again, doing a poor impersonation of Alan.

"Dr. Grant!" Hammond gasped.

Lex stood, strolled a few paces away from the table and sent a fast ball hurtling toward the garishly painted radio. "This is boring!" she proclaimed as it flew to pieces.

Timmy fought back unruly tears, she could be so insensitive. "I'll get us some snacks, then," he said stiffly.

Lex turned up her Walkman and as Timmy neared the freezer 'mmmbop' receded into blackness. Timmy pressed the big red button that disengaged the heavy freezer door. Inside the air was surprisingly cold and Timmy wished, not for the last time, that he'd brought a warmer jacket. Once his weary eyes fell on the Froyo, a ruckus sounded outside in the dining hall.

"Oh my lord! The velociraptors are here!" Lex yelled, indicating they weren't alone. Puzzled, Timmy slipped from the freezer to investigate. He heard a short squeal then a jagged ripping and crunch.

"Lex??"

There was silence, then, tentative and whispery, "Hello. It is me, legs."

"What are you talking about!? Did you fall and hurt your legs? Answer me Lex!"

"My name is Lex."

"Oh okay. Wait a minute, you're a velociraptor!"

"Yes, we can talk now."

Timmy turned to run, but he was too slow. The Raptors had fitted themselves with JP Inline skates and were gaining on him easily, and in style. The thick hard plastic reflected the moonlight. Underneath, four deadly yellow wheels rolled irrevocably onward.

"We're not going to eat you!" they insisted, tongues lolling wildly, flinging their rancid saliva, "we're going to take you on a shopping spree!"

Timmy ducked into the kitchen and crouched against a tall pots n pans rack. Suddenly one of the raptors crashed into the rack, sending kitchen ware into the air. "Makeover!" it hissed madly.

Fiercely, one of them slammed a tawny wig onto his head. They gathered in around him and savagely applied foundation, then eyeliner. "Yes. Yes! More!" the ringleader squealed, viciously lathering on the blush. They threw a cheap dress over the whole ordeal and the process was complete.

Slowly, Timmy trailed to the window. His reflection hung in the night air. "I look like Dolly Parton on crystal meth," he said.

"Then our work is complete," and they were never seen, on Earth, again.

# DRIFT

## JEFFREY SYKES

I stretched the mic cable into the darkness and began to re-
cite Lincoln's Gettysburg Address so Dooley could check the
levels back at the truck. We'd set the four-track on the lowered
tailgate a few minutes earlier. Now, Anne and I were twenty feet
out toward a series of ledges that led down to the banks of the
Tuckaseegee River.

"Four score and seven years ago," I whispered into the mic and
looked back to Dooley. He gave me thumbs up, signaling the
levels were good. Anne and I looked out across the land rip-
pling down toward the river. We stood silent in the July darkness
listening to the cicadas. A lone car whisked around the curve
on the state road behind us before disappearing down the
mountainside.

"What are we listening for?" Anne asked.

"This," I said as I guided my hand out over the valley floor toward the hill that rose on the other side of the river. It made a
borderline in the darkness separating earth from sky. I held the
microphone out in front of me and grabbed Anne by the waist,
pulling her close to me again.

I let my hand drift down her hip, just below her skirt, and ran my fingers along the smooth surface of her thigh. Anne leaned her head on my shoulder and sighed.

We stood face to face in the darkness twenty minutes earlier in the middle of the short gravel drive that led to my basement apartment. She'd moved in upstairs a month before. I'd been living here a week longer. A friend had tipped me off to the duplex, a two minute walk from the edge of campus along Centennial Drive.

It was the second summer term and campus was dead. Traffic along the road just above my place was sparse. As Anne and I stood in the warm July night she leaned in to me. We'd begun to kiss and I moved my hand below the pleated hem of her short skirt. She hadn't flinched and soon I found my fingers running along the edge of her panty line to play softly with the damp, inviting flesh below.

She'd just moaned into my ear and wrapped her hand around the back of my neck when I saw the headlights veer off the road and angle down toward where we stood.

My acoustic Fender guitar hung from my shoulder, with the body of the guitar around the back, the strap across my chest. Anne and I pulled apart and I reached behind me to grab the tip of the neck, bringing the dreadnought body out front.

The truck came closer and I could see that it was Dooley. It wasn't yet 9:30, but since I was known to be single and always welcomingg to a friend, it was nothing strange for people to stop by late if the lights were on.

I would soon learn to turn them off early.

I couldn't be too upset with Dooley. He'd been a good friend for the three years I'd been at university and I knew he was lonely. His girlfriend of two years, Christy, had left him sometime after spring break. Dooley's normal countenance was dour but over the last few months he'd been especially morose.

I finger picked a bluesy D-7 chord and vamped to an A as I heard his emergency brake ratchet up and the headlights died. Anne leaned against the quarter panel of my Volkswagen and fidgeted with her nails.

"What's up, Dooley? Out late this evening," I said as he walked closer. I picked out a little run to end the tune.

"Yeah, man. How's it going over here? Working on a new song are you?"

"Oh you know it brother. All the time," I replied. "As a matter of fact, Anne of Green Gables and I were just about to strike up a tune when you pulled up. What were we going to sing about GG?"

Anne rolled her eyes and laughed. "You have got to stop making up names for me Steven. I can't keep them all straight."

"Some habits die hard," I said. "Especially when you're a poet. Words just seem to flow from my tongue at times. Tends to get me in trouble."

We shared a laugh but Dooley wasn't fazed. I could tell he wanted something.

"Say man I tried to call Eric, and then Peyton, but none of them are around. You know where I can score a bag?"

This put me in a tight spot. If he hadn't been among my closest circle of friends, and the guy who played bass in my fledgling psychedelic rock band, I would have been pissed at him. Anne and I had only known each other about two weeks, since the time she heard me playing guitar on the stone steps along the side of the house.

I was playing a new chord scheme and humming, then scatting, some lyrical rhythms, when Anne appeared at the top of the steps.

I hadn't had cause to tell her all my secrets. I surely hadn't told her about the weed connection I'd developed that spring. In fact,

I didn't like to deal out of the house at all. I preferred to roll out to a friend's house to deliver and catch a smoke. I wasn't dealing large quantities, just a handful of quarters and twenty dollar sacks for friends in order to make my smoke quota.

But I had a feeling Anne was ok. We'd smoked a few times together and giggled in her living room watching Beevis and Butthead. Tonight was the first time I'd kissed her, but I figured we might soon have little, if anything, between us. So I let Dooley's gaffe slide.

"Well now Dooley, what kind of question is that to ask a guy standing in the middle of the driveway? Let's go inside. I need a cigarette."

I reached out for Anne's fingertips and she moved the rest of her hand into mine. I led her toward the muted yellow glow coming from behind the antique glaze of the single pane windows at my doorway and Dooley fell in behind us. I slid my arm around Anne's shoulders and then let her go first up the two steps to the porch and into the small living room.

I moved my Gibson SG from the chair and put it in the worn black case leaning in the corner. I grabbed up my lyrics notebook and chord sheets from the coffee table and placed them next to the four-track. Anne took a seat in the space I just created and picked up the Electric Ladyland tab book sitting on the coffee table. Dooley sat on the couch, leaving me standing in the room still holding the acoustic. With nowhere to put it down I thought it was a good opportunity to go in the back room and get a sack ready for Dooley.

"Let me put this guitar up in its case," I said and stepped into the narrow hallway and took a few steps around a corner to the bedroom. I didn't have a case for that guitar because I'd purchased it at a pawn shop earlier that summer. So I leaned it in the corner and opened the third drawer on my dresser. I still had four quarter bags, two twenty sacks and my personal stash from the last quarter pound Peyton had fronted me earlier in the week. It was heavy on shake with a few seeds and that had pissed me off good, but at the price he was letting it go for I could easily move it for $30 a quarter and smoke most of the shake.

I'd been enjoying the taste of joints that summer and so shake was ok with me. A few of my regulars had mentioned how the quality was less than stellar, but it was the middle of the summer and weed was hard to come by. I just wanted to get stoned on the cheap so I didn't really care what they thought. I stuffed one of the quarters in my shorts and grabbed my personal stash.

At the doorway to the living room I paused.

"Anyone want a beer? Anne, can I get you something?"

She nodded and Dooley got up to follow me into the kitchen. I pulled a few Becks from the refrigerator and had set them on the slate gray countertops as Dooley came in the room. After I fumbled for the bottle opener I looked at him.

"Keep your voice down," I whispered. "I don't want her knowing I keep weed in the house to sell. I don't know her roommate that well. She's a local, kind of uppity toward me." I put the bag up on the counter. "Put this in your pocket. We'll smoke a joint in a minute but don't say anything about that bag."

"How much, man?"

"Thirty," I said and he handed me three wrinkled tens.

As I popped the bottle tops I called to Anne.

"You want a glass, GG?"

"No," came the reply with a hint of laughter. "Bottle's fine."

Back in the living room I sat on the couch next to Dooley. It was perpendicular to the chair, my chair, which Anne sat in now. She still thumbed through the Hendrix tab book.

"Do you like that album?" I asked. She said she wasn't familiar with it. "Oh my God. We will have to rectify that tonight. It's an amazing album. Has to be my favorite from beginning to end. Hendrix and Eddie Kramer did wonders with stereo pan and early attempts at delay with vocals and pitch modulation. It's fascinating."

I lit the finger-sized joint and after getting it going passed it over to Anne. I leaned back into the couch and exhaled the smoke. It cast a shroud in the dim light coming from the fixture in the ceiling.

"In fact, I've been experimenting with delay and pitch modulation this week. I got a friend's Microsynth and hooked it up to the digital delay pedal... It's the blue double switched one next to the four track."

I pointed to the makeshift counter I'd put together. It consisted of a large black trunk covered with a tie-dyed sheet that I'd picked up somewhere along the way. The trunk rested atop four milk crates stacked in pairs of two so it was just high enough to be at chest level when I was in a chair.

"I run the guitar signal into the Microsynth and then put that into the delay pedal. Then I send the out on the delay into whatever track is open on the four." The joint had come back to me and I pulled on the moist tip of white paper and let the sensation fill my lungs. Purple flowers. A wisp of the fragrance you'd catch on a mountain path early on a cool afternoon. The ember gave off a heavy stack of smoke and I leaned in to pull the remnants from the air with my nose. I held the substance in my expanded lungs and passed the half-smoked spliff over to Dooley.

I moved over to the stool in front of my workstation and exhaled once I sat down.

"I've been closing in on some Fripp and Eno type sounds today. Simple phrases I can overdub with solo work."

"Can we hear it?" Anne asked.

"I don't have any speakers but I can play it for you on the phones. Let me get it going."

She smiled as her soft brown eyes looked up to me. I rewound the tape back to zero and thought of the afternoon's bliss as

I developed the piece from a three note phrase, modulated by the filters and oscillators on the Microsynth. Once I was happy with it I had clicked the digital delay's infinite repeat button and spent an hour adjusting the controls, cutting the repetitions as I slowed the meter of the phrase itself, processing the original notes into something worlds apart from the moment of creation.

Anne listened to the sketch I'd created that afternoon and we polished off the smoke. She bailed first, a wave of the hand signaling "enough." Dooley and I took a few more turns until he said "No man, I'm good" and I set the roach down in the ashtray to join the dozen already there.

It was only about 10 o'clock now and that particular interaction of fire, marijuana and white paper had fused the room with a pulsating energy. I can't say that my music had anything to do with it. Quite the contrary, it was a slow, spacey piece I'd tentatively titled "Cosmic Engine Failure" because toward the end I'd had the vision of a spaceship crashing on a desolate planet.

When Anne finished listening we all seemed to feel the need to get up and move. Maybe it was the weed. Maybe it was the tension in the room with one person too many being present.

I suggested we take the four track and a mic outside to capture atmospheric sounds so I could use them to augment the piece. No one hesitated and I felt that if we spent an hour or so outside Dooley would get the picture and take off. That would leave plenty of time for the evening's activity to run its course.

In the darkness you could not see the Mountain Laurel or the orange tipped Tiger Lilies lining the hillside separating my driveway from the road above. But in the cool stillness that surrounded us you could smell the bountiful fragrance nature offered this night.

I ran an extension cord from the living room to the bed of the truck and moved the four track there. I grabbed one mic and a cable and was back outside before Dooley had time to get his bearings.

"What are we doing exactly, man?" he said after taking a pull from the green beer bottle in his hand.

"Recording the life of this particular evening, Dooley. Just for a few minutes. I want to get some atmospherics on tape so I can experiment with them tomorrow. You got time to help me with that dontcha?"

"Sure man, anything for you Steve."

His blithe tone came close to hitting that raw nerve in me that triggers aggression. But just as I was about to vent on him I remembered all he'd been through in the last few months. The breakup with Christy, the extra strength sadness, how he'd tried to sabotage a relationship I had with a curvaceous local girl not more than two months ago. But we'd been friends for too long for me to let that come between us. I'd been sad before. I'd known the weight of solitary confinement. And so I'd let that slide too.

But our relationship was drifting. If I hadn't needed him to round out the band I so desperately wanted to be in, we would've seen less and less of each other. In fact, back in April he'd asked me why I hadn't been coming around and I told him straight up that it was all I could do not to hit him for the way he'd come between me and Marie right after Christy dumped him.

In early spring I'd moved out of the popular A-frame party spot where my band's drummer Dewey lived. The house was too active. Too many people coming and going. And too much distraction as I'd tried to salvage my relationship with Marie after a fit of jealousy led to rage on my part.

Dooley took my spot in the rotation and as I tried to make a new scene for myself I only popped by for band practice and to occasionally hang with Dewey. One day after classes and our obligatory afternoon buzz I was running scales on Dooley's small organ he'd moved into the A-frame. Dewey took off to run errands and I'd stayed behind to work out some melodies that'd been running in my head for a few days.

A short time later Dooley came back from campus, and after exchanging the quietest of greetings, we passed fifteen minutes without speaking. But music had always pulled us together. After he got a taste of the major seven and ninth chords I was working out, he came and sat on a stool next to the organ.

We made light small talk for a bit until he'd commented about it being nice to see me come around. I'd been holding in the bitterness toward him for weeks, and I let it out as I stood up, kicked the stool across the room and stomped out the door.

He tried to play like he didn't know what he was doing, with his self-deprecation and constant passive aggressive posturing. We'd been close before and I knew he wasn't simple. So I figured manipulation, like a composer lulling you into comfort before flipping it back around, was his game. And after Marie and I eased back the intensity a few notches, he was on her like a scale resolving to its root.

But Marie and I hadn't split up completely. We still spent time together in the afternoons and often made love in the evenings before I took her back to her mom's shotgun shack one block east of the paper mill that dominated the small town a few miles away from campus. She told me how she'd been at the A-frame with some mutual friends and how Dooley got her off in the dining room alone and tried to serenade her with the Pink Floyd song that'd been the foundation of our relationship. I knew what his game was.

Marie and I tried to work the kinks out of our affair and I went all in, shutting off everything but school, band and Marie. But she didn't go to school. She was a local, but wildly popular in our underground set. I didn't know it at the time but in those last few weeks she was using me, trading the occasional physical act for a ride or a buzz or a meal to get her through the cyclical lull in her life before another glorious summer rolled around.

And so it was about the middle of May that we stopped seeing each other much more than once a week. I knew in my heart she was seeing someone else and so I made the decision to let go.

See, I'd been a 20-year old virgin prior to the night in my bedroom that past year when I flipped Marie back down onto the bed as she tried to break off our make out session. There was a full blown party downstairs and when she'd said "no they'll hear us" I said "bullshit there's twenty people partying downstairs" and had my moment in the sun.

It had been very hard for me to come to grips with the disconnect between sex and love. But as Marie and I drifted apart, I began to grow beyond my mother's working class Christianity that haunted a certain small region of my brain. And just as I did, the floodgates opened.

Cara had been up first, about a week after I moved into my current apartment. Dewey, Dooley and I had played the second slot of a huge house party. When we came off stage about 11:30 that night, Cara was standing there and came right up to me. What she whispered in my ear still gives me a shiver after all this time. The things we did that first night and the three other nights we spent together in June are a wellspring of joy that I've only tried to describe to someone once. But the words failed me.

I had noticed that same glint in Anne's eyes after the first few times we hung together in her living room watching MTV after her roommate went to work. And so as I'd found myself standing face to face with her in my driveway this evening, I didn't hesitate to see what was what.

But Dooley.

I led Anne around the yard from the native rhododendrons at the edge of the driveway to the base of the poplar tree at the corner of the house. I held the microphone out to get the crunch of our feet on the increasingly damp grass along the side of the gravel drive. I drifted my hand across the rich verdant texture of the rhododendron leaves and let the mic capture the soft rustle of friction. I pointed it to the sky as a tick hound barked in the distance across the river.

Anne and I began to whisper gibberish into the mic and she giggled as I moved it back and forth between her mouth and mine.

After a few minutes I looked over to the truck and saw Dooley had finished with his beer. Anne and I made our way over to him as I carefully coiled up the slackened mic cable.

"Well that ought to be enough," I said. "Thanks Dooley."

"Hey no problem," he said, passionless. "I appreciate you letting me hang out here for a bit, but I guess I'll head on home now. Thanks for the beer and all."

I caught the hint of his defeatism but wasn't biting.

"Don't go Dooley. You sure you don't want another beer? We could get a few more extension cords from inside or daisy chain the mic cables and see how close we can get down to the river ..."

Anne kicked me in the leg. She didn't know I was fucking with him.

"No man, I appreciate it but I guess I'll head on home and see about getting to bed."

I gathered up the four track and took it back inside as Dooley pulled off back up the driveway before making a two point turn in order to get pointed in the right direction home.

I was just gathering the extension cord up when Anne spoke.

"He seems like such a sad person. What's the matter with him?"

"Dooley has always been dour, GG. I don't know if it's the drugs or something from his family life. He's as smart as anyone and has been known to have a good sense of wit, but he's morose more often than not."

"That's too bad for him."

"Yeah and it doesn't help that his girlfriend dumped his sour ass back in March. He's been insufferable since then."

"Who was she?"

"You saw her here a few nights last week. Christy is her name. She's the tall, really white skinned girl. You'd like her. She's from up north just like you. She drives that maroon Chrysler van. She and Dooley lived together the last two years. I'm not sure what happened, if she got tired of him or what. I think she's moved out to her own place on the other side of campus, down River Road."

Anne was leaning on my Volkswagen and looking out across the night.

"I'll put this cable up. You want another beer or anything? I could do with one."

She smiled. "That would be good, but I'm going to go upstairs first for a few minutes. I'll be right back. Can you wait for me?"

"Certainly," I said.

She bopped up the stone stairs into the darkness and I took the bottles and the extension cord inside. In the kitchen I was pulling out two more bottles and wondering if I was being naive or if I was moving toward the third act. I thought briefly about my parents, the finalized divorce, my mother's middle aged sadness and my father's timely advice about not getting married. Ever.

Back outside, the clarity of the stars was brilliant as I looked between the heavy leaved trees to make out part of the Big Dipper. The handle stuck up high in the darkness as the edge of the dipper was hidden behind a ridgeline.

Anne came back quickly and after we sipped the beers for a few minutes I took hers and set it over on the porch. As I kissed her softly, tasting the husky remnants of cigarette and other smoke amidst her freshly brushed teeth, she ground into me and whispered "let's go inside."

I widened the disconnect between sex and love that week. It was as if I'd placed an ad or a billboard that screamed "will fuck for fun". It was like I'd repented of all my slavish fears about my body and my mother's morality and what it all meant in the long run.

For about two weeks I alternated between Cara and Anne in what seemed like an infinite loop of lust. Anne made it clear that first night after we came inside that while she was with me then, she might just want to be with one of my friends next. Cara would call me from her job at a group home for troubled teens and arrange a meeting place for after dark. She'd dated an acquaintance of mine for about a year and was working her way out of a living arrangement with him.

"I'm not looking for a relationship with you," she'd say on the phone. Our second night together I was supposed to pick her up in a gravel parking lot behind an area where road crews stored materials for patch repair. She didn't want anyone to see her car at my place just yet. We started in to each other in the pitch black of midnight once we got back inside. By the time the sun came up and soft light filtered across her face, sweat bonded us together. In the shower an hour later we made love again and I understood that momentary bliss would never be exceeded.

More than fifteen years later my mother died suddenly from a stroke. Amidst the wreckage of her final years, in a small trailer where she'd isolated herself as she tried to hide from youthful shame she'd never truly shed, I found a set of pictures stuffed deep in a dented two-drawer filing cabinet.

Because of the suddenness of her death, and the paralysis of grief that gripped my sister and me, we made choices on the fly about what to keep and what to throw away. I wanted pictures and a few other mementos from my childhood–a ceramic Santa Claus she'd made, a framed needlepoint with the words "houses are made of bricks and stones, but homes are made love alone"–and I stuffed these items in the small cardboard box my uncle secured from the liquor store down the road.

Months later, as I was sorting through the box after grief turned to guilt, and I needed to bathe in her memory, I was gripped by a set of photos. My mother out west with a half-brother she never knew existed. A dazed vacancy on her face as she looks at the camera. It's a year after my parent's divorce. She is forty-five years old.

One of the photos is of an overcast sky, a down quilt of clouds taken from her seat on an airplane. The grayness somewhat blurred by the motion and the mistimed shutter speed. A metaphor of the vagaries tormenting a life spent searching for clarity. I feel the grief that she endured in those days as the certainty of her lineage fell apart the same way her marriage had only recently as well.

I pondered over the gray stillness of the clouds–beautiful but tinged with sadness, as if there to hide the beauty of firmament from those put on this earth to suffer. I could see my mother taking the picture from her window seat on the cross-continental flight, but I wondered did she capture the moment on the way to Seattle or as she left to return east?

I flipped the picture over as another tear traced the now double-circled wrinkles of my once youthful eye. On the back in computer print the words "July/August 1993". A hollow pain emptied my stomach as I thought about how alone she must have felt then. I sat down in my chair and stared at the words and then the picture again and remembered how Dooley had hanged himself during that first week of August after Christy asked if she could spend the night with me.

I didn't even think twice about saying yes to her.

# DAYS FOR THE RAIN

## JIM DOERING

It started out a sunny autumn day, which meant I got to walk in the garden. White and lavender crocuses grow where the path turns toward a small pond. Miss Anderson walked with me one day and said, "You know, Kayla, when crocuses grow at Easter, they represent Christ on the cross coming back from the dead for your sins and mine." I'd like to believe her, except I don't know if she has any real sins at all. She's nice to me, and listens when I want to talk. I've never heard her say a bad thing about anybody, or seen her do anything mean to them either. I have my sins all right, but I'm keeping them to myself.

There are tiny frogs that sit on dark green lily pads in the pond. They're my friends. They talk to me and keep me company while I sit and read on the concrete bench near the edge of the water. A little creek flows into the pond. It keeps it full year round. I like the sound of the water trickling over the rocks. I'd stay there all day if I could, but I never get to stay as long as I want.

One day when the crocuses were in bloom, I picked one on my way back to the main building and took it with me. I put it in a little plastic cup on top of my dresser. After it died, I put the dead flower in a cardboard box in the bottom drawer of the dresser underneath my pants. I called it my flower coffin.

Phoebe was in my room one day and asked why I liked crocuses so much. I told her I didn't like them, but she didn't believe me. She wouldn't leave me alone, and kept asking until I stopped talking to her. That's when she gave up, nodded at me and said, "Okay girl," and went back to her room with her hands stuck in the pockets of her blue jumper. She does that sometimes when she's mad.

At group, Mrs. Ordonez asked each of us if there was anything we wanted to talk about. When it was my turn, I told her there wasn't anything I needed to share. She said that I could have time if anything came to me. A little later I thought of something so I raised my hand. I told the group how I hated when it wasn't raining. Some of the girls looked at me oddly. A few laughed and made sarcastic comments. Mrs. Ordonez shushed them and told me to go ahead and tell them why.

"When it rains, it's quiet," I said. My voice came out almost like a whisper.

Maizie yelled, "You is one stupid crazy bitch, Kayla. Thunderstorms is really loud." Maizie hates me. She's bigger than me, but I'm not scared of her. Some of the girls are afraid because she hurts them sometimes.

Mrs. Ordonez turned to Maizie and said, "That will be quite enough." Then she looked at me and said, "How does the rain make it quieter, Kayla? Help us to understand."

I looked around the room. Everybody stared at me and I felt weird, but Mrs. Ordonez smiled and said it was okay. "When it rains, I can't hear Phoebe screaming, or the other girls crying, or Maizie yelling at me from down the hall that she's going to kill me when I go to sleep. When it rains, it gets a lot quieter in my head because I can't hear anybody but me."

Nobody said anything for a long time. Finally Mrs. Ordonez called on another girl who talked about how mad she was at her parents. Walking out of the room after group, Mrs. Ordonez put her arm around me and gave me a hug like I was her own kid or something, even though I'm nobody's kid anymore.

The next day it was a lot colder, and when I walked to the pond with my book, all my frog friends were gone. Do frogs go south for the winter? I hope so, because I would hate to think what would happen when the pond froze over and my friends didn't go somewhere warm. I didn't stay very long. The wind whipped up and I was cold even with my jacket. On my way back, I saw there was only one live crocus blossom left, so I squatted down and picked it. While I was at it, I picked all the dead ones too. There were lots of them, so I stuffed them into both pockets of my jumper.

After I took my meds, I saw Miss Anderson talking to a new lady. I tried to mind my own business, but when I passed by, they both looked at me and Miss Anderson whispered, "Mishandled" and "Abused." I walked away as quickly as I could. I didn't want to hear any more, and the voices in my head were screaming at me. I wished it was raining so I didn't have to think.

Back in my room, I took the dead flower out of the cup and put in the last live one. The dead one went to join its brothers and sisters, including the ones in my pockets. In a day or two the new one will be dead too, but I didn't mind.

A couple days ago a new girl arrived and said that tomorrow there's supposed to be snow. I don't much like snow. I lay down on my bed and imagined loud rainy days, but the bad thoughts snuck back into my head anyway. When the last crocus flower dies, I'll have over fifty. In one of my books I read that crocus flowers can make you sick if you eat them, and if you consume a lot they can actually kill you. I wonder if that book is right.

# ENGLISH GARDEN

## FREEDOM CHEVALIER

Malcolm smiled with satisfaction as he gazed out upon his English garden, warming in the California sun. He had long since left his home in the Cotswold region and had promised that when time and money permitted, he would recreate his childhood garden; but this time with Azaleas. His mother hated Azaleas. They now framed the perimeter of his lustrous beachfront home. She'd hate what I've done to this place, he thought smugly to himself as he stepped over her resting place.

He'd planted the largest Azalea bush on top of the moist patch of soil where her ashes were scattered, and left a dish of premium kibble out for the few neighborhood strays, enticing them to claim their territory. Azaleas and cat piss. How do I love you, mother, let me count the ways.

It had been a lovely funeral. The Monsignor at the Church of the Suffering Souls seemed taken aback when Malcolm asked him to oversee the opulent service.

"My mother was a lifelong Catholic." Malcolm professed, with thespian perfect tears, "It would mean so much to her, to know her soul would forever rest with our Lord." Knowing his mother's outright contempt and hatred of the Catholic Church made it a challenge to keep the smile licking at the corners of his full lips from showing. He bit the inside of his cheek for control and allowed fresh tears to burn the rim of his steel blue eyes.

"I understand your grief, my son," the kindly old believer offered.

He had used not a small portion of his inheritance already. The funeral, the wake, the garden. And Michael. Money well spent.

He padded into the back bedroom and watched as the dense musculature of Michael's back seemed to crash and surge, even as the younger man slept. His mother's bed. Fresh linens of course and a new headboard, but it was still hers.

He had watched Michael scale the Malibu surf for several weeks prior to his mother's death; from this very room. After delivering her breakfast at precisely 8:15 A.M. on one of those last mornings, he lost himself staring out the big bay window.

"Malcolm!" She screamed, shattering his reverie. Hearing his name screeched, he turned too quickly displaying a prominent tent at the crotch of his beige Dockers. His face flushed and his heartbeat thundered in his ears. His knees rubbered, screaming their inability to support his tubby physique and he fought to steady himself against the rail on her bed.

"Disgusting," she condemned. "You're pathetic!" Her final verdict, absolute.

"Yes, Mother," Malcolm apologized, not raising his gaze as he left the room.

"I won't have it! I want curtains! Thick black curtains covering these windows. This afternoon!" She demanded. "Something that blocks the window. I don't want you coming in here pretending to be interested in me, just because you're horny. Damn fool. I won't have it!"

"Yes, Mother," was all Malcolm managed in response.

"Something to stop this immorality. I won't have it! Not in my house!"

He had complied without objection knowing it to be the only way to shut her up. That or kill her, of course.


He sat at his desk and wrote the monthly checks for the nurse, prescriptions, the physical therapist. It was costing so much to keep her alive, he mused, and quickly admonished himself for such a thought. She was his mother, he owed her so much... didn't he?

"Malcolm!" She cawed. "What are you doing now?"

"The books, mother," he replied walking, into her room.

"They should have been done by now."

"Yes, Mother."

"You're too lazy."

"I know mother."

"You're so incompetent! I'm surprised you haven't killed me yet."

"Yes mother." He let his head sag, the pepper-salt whiskers on his chin brushing against his button-down sky blue collar. *Don't think such things, Malcolm.*


He folded the ironing board with care, ensuring it did not make the scratching sound that annoyed his mother so, and placed it back in the linen closet. He waited for the iron to cool and returned it to its place atop the fridge, turning its handle outward to line up against the edge. He smiled at his stack of freshly ironed shirts and trousers. They were still warm as he carried them into his room and put them into their appropriate drawers, one at a time; smoothing each one as he did.

He caught his reflection in the mirror and noticed the slight upturn of hair against the back of his collar. He'd have to get a haircut this afternoon, before his mother saw it. He didn't want to shave his head again. He had learned her lesson well the last time.

"Are you writing it all down, Malcolm?" His mother shot at him.

"Yes, mother."

"Are you sure you're getting it all?"

"Yes, mother."

"You're getting it all wrong. I just know it. You can't get anything right! You there, check his notes!" She demanded of the new nurse. They were usually new. They didn't tend to stay long, but Malcolm didn't blame them.

Yukiko smiled and bowed slightly, still not yet fully removed from her traditional upbringing.

"He has taken excellent notes." She assured.

"Fucking foreigners." His mother condemned, "Always kissing ass."

Malcolm offered a knowing smile in an attempt to assuage the sting. Yukiko nodded and continued her instructions on how to use the new oxygen machine.

"It is very important to keep it attached here." Yukiko's slender finger traced along the row of flashing buttons, radial dials and input valves. "You can feel it click when it's in place." She reached out and guided Malcolm's hand to the machine. His hand looked fat and bulbous in hers. He blushed just enough to pink his pale jowls, and hoped she wouldn't notice. It had been a long time since anyone had touched him so gently. Malcolm found the brush of skin against skin, stirring.

"If it disconnects, your okaasan, oh sorry, your mother," she smiled self-consciously correcting her English, "your mother will not get enough oxygen. You will need to check it before bed, and during the night. It could pull out if she moves too much in her sleep."

*It could pull out if she moves too much in her sleep.*


The doorbell detonated in the perfectly still house, causing Malcolm to jump at its explosive peal. He had been engrossed in the most recent issue of Architects Journal (UK) and spilled his chamomile tea, soaking the first ten pages.

*I'm coming, I'm coming, don't ring the bell ag…*

He hadn't finished the thought before the bell sounded a second time, rousing his mother.

"Who's at the goddamned door, Malcolm?"

"I don't know, mother." He called back. "I'll check."

"Well, get rid of them!"

"Yes, mother." Malcolm sighed.

He opened the door a crack, just enough to see the man from the back window beach standing at his door. Michael was wearing a black swim brief by California Muscle, clinging even tighter than designed thanks to the sea water that dripped down his shoulder length sun-bleached hair, across his immense golden chest, over taut rippled abs, diverting at his belly button into twin rivulets that vanished at the waistband and its half tied drawstring above a glistening, prominent -

"Um, yes, can I, um, help you?" Malcolm stumbled.

"He yours?" Michael asked of the squirming bundle of puppy he held carefully in his colossal bronze arms.

Malcolm carefully stepped onto the porch, closing the door behind him blocking his mother's crescive rage. Bending into the little dog's collar he read his neighbor's address.

"It looks like he belongs to Melody. She lives there." He pointed to next house over. "She must have a new dog. Her other dog, Prada, passed away last winter. You must be thirsty, "he said, bending to the little dog. "Do you want to come in for some water…for the puppy."

"Who is it? What's going on Malcolm?" his mother called out.

"It's okay, Mother."

"I can hear someone. Who's out there?"

"It's nothing, Mother."

"Don't tell me it's nothing! I can hear someone."

"Will you excuse me a moment?" Malcolm asked of Michael, while the young pup greedily lapped and splashed water over the kitchen floor. "That's Mother. She's not well."

Malcolm went to his Mother's room. "We have company, Mother. A young dog was loose. They thought he was ours. He belongs to Melody. I've given the dog some water. They'll be leaving."

"You let a dog drink out of my dishes? You better get me new dishes. I don't eat out of dog bowls! Get rid of them. Now! Get that dog out of here!"

"Yes, Mother."

"This is quite the spread you've got here." Michael said on Malcolm's return.

"It's Mother's, really. She's not well."

Silence hung between the two men while the dog chased dust motes dancing in a sunbeam. Malcolm caught Michael's smoky grey eyes, and he smiled self-consciously. Malcolm shifted from foot to foot, uncertain of what to say next. Before he could decide, the dog shattered the awkward silence with a joyful *yelp*.

"I should probably bring him next door."

"Yes. Melody is very sweet. She'll be most grateful." Malcolm walked Michael and the dog to the door.

"You should come down to sometime. You surf?"

"No."

"You should try."

"I can't surf."

"You ever try before?"

"No."

"Then how do you know you can't do it!" Michael slapped Malcolm's arm playfully. "Hey, you're hiding some muscle under there, aren't ya?"

"I have to lift Mother out of the bed. She's not well." Malcolm's face fell, unable to say more.

"Well, you know where to find me. C'mon little dude, let's get you home." Michael turned and jogged the short distance to Melody's place. Malcolm watched through the corner window as Melody embraced both Michael and the young rebellious pup; pulling them both into the foyer and out of his line of sight.

"Did you get rid of that mutt?"

"Yes, Mother."

"Then get in here and clean up this shit."

Malcolm took a slow deep breath, and steeled himself before opening the door to his mother's room. She had thrown her water glass against the window; its shards sparkling in the afternoon sun, just beginning to creep in through the window. She had overturned her lunch tray sending the remnants of the lobster bisque across the room, splattering the green walls with Pollack-esque stains. She had removed her diaper, after an abnormally prodigious dump and slapped it against the wall directly behind her, wiping it back and forth a few times before letting it slide down behind her bed, coming to a foul stop against the freshly painted the floor trim.

She had thrashed so much she had pulled her breathing tube component nearly out of its attachment.

"You should be more careful, Mother," Malcolm offered. "You could have died."

"Oh, you'd just love that wouldn't you? You'd be a mess without me, you know that. I keep you respectable! Can you imagine your life, without me here?"

*Mother, you could have died.*

*Can you imagine your life, without me here!*


"Dinner, Mother."

He waited for a reply to his knock on her bedroom door, just slightly ajar. Nothing.

"I made a Spinach salad tonight, for something different."

He pushed the door open with his shoulder. He placed the tray on the bedside stand and looked down at his mother, sleeping; still. So still. *So very still.* He watched her chest for movement, not certain if he was actually seeing her breathe or if his eyes were playing tricks on him. He leaned in closer. Listening.

"Get off of me!" She shouted into his ear, causing him to jump with surprise. "What, you thought I was dead? I'm not dead. Get off of me!"

Malcolm struggled to regain his footing and his composure.

"I'm sorry, Mother."

He pinched the bridge of his nose and took a deep, controlled breath. Exhaling, he brought the tray of food over for her to eat.

"What the hell is this?"

"It's spinach. I thought it might nice to have something a little different."

"I don't like it."

"But you haven't tried it. How do you know you don't like it?" Malcolm smiled to himself, remembering his earlier conversation with Michael.

"I know I don't like it, because I don't like it! God, you're an idiot!" She tossed the dish aside. "And clean that up before you go."

"Yes, Mother."


Malcolm was jolted awake by the crashing of dark, rabid waves against the rocks below. His window strained against the savage pelting rain and unyielding winds. Thunder rolled, tympanic. Lightening ripped at the night sky, illuminating his room. He found his slippers without challenge, despite the power outage.

"Coming, Mother." Malcolm replied to no call. "I'll be right there."

He wrapped his robe tightly around his waist and made the short trip to the room next door.

"The power's gone." He said as he opened her door and saw her on the bed, writhing. Her yellowing eyes widened as she clawed at her throat.

He thought he saw her lips form the word *breathe*. He strained to listen, but couldn't hear her over the storm slamming into the house. She grabbed at the air as she tried to extend a pale, bony hand toward him, but only ended up pulling the oxygen tube across her neck, out from under her nose.

Malcolm took a step into her room, but stopped when he saw the machine; the continuous metronomic click-click deafeningly absent. And the festive array of brightly blinking red and yellow lights, barely held on to the remnants of a sickly amber glow in the dark and shadowy corner of the old woman's room. The backup battery had failed to kick in and the essential oxygen feed that would keep his beloved mother alive and with him for at least another ten years, or so her specialists believed, had ceased. Another clap of thunder. Another slash across the ocean sky illuminated his mother's contorted, twisted face as she gasped and grasped at air in the black-blue night.

Her eyes were wild now. Pitch-colored saucers that reflected the oceans' rage. Her mouth opened and closed in futile attempts to capture any amount of oxygen. Malcolm was reminded of the time he had gone fishing with friends and landed a large silver and black striped bass. It had flopped at his feet on the boat, dying. They stood watching for a moment; then without a single word, placed the fish back into the sun dappled water with care. They up-ended their bait jars in the same spot and sailed back to shore in silence.

He could see bubbles of spit forming at the corners of her mouth as she tried to speak, or breathe, he wasn't certain which. She had kicked with such violence that the guardrail closest to him was detached and hanging down on one side, allowing most of the blankets to slide off into a small mound. She would want them washed tomorrow, he thought to himself.

"Yes, Mother." Malcolm answered as he backed out of the room, closing the door with care. He waited outside listening for the machine to turn back on, the back-up battery to kick in, but nothing happened.

The storm swelled, battering the house. A dead <u>thud</u> hammered the roof and slowly scraped its way over the edge, buffeted by the howling winds, causing Malcolm to tremble.

He walked back to his room, closed his door, removed his slippers and crawled back into bed. He pulled the duvet up and over his head like a child. Exhausted, he fell into a deep, uninterrupted sleep and remained there until morning.

The parade of emergency personnel, police, fire and ambulance, along with throngs of rubbernecking onlookers, caused Malcolm to feel strangely blithe the following morning. The effulgent southern California sun shown down with all the brightness it could muster in honour of the jubilant occasion. Melody came by, walking Snowball on a new leash, to see if she could help. He assured her that he was fine. He saw Michael's gentle smile at the fringes of the mushrooming crowd, standing against a freshly waxed surf board; his hair pulled into a loose ponytail that seemed to magnify the depth of his eyes. Malcolm smiled a little in return, allowing his usual reticence to recede for an awkward moment.

"I'm very sorry for your loss," an official from the coroner's office was saying as they loaded his mother into the ambulance. "There will be papers for you to sign."

"Of course."

"You can bring them down. We have a counsellor, who can help with the funeral arrangements."

"It's all taken care of. Mother was very well organized."

"Burial? Or cremation?"

She had wanted to be buried. She had bought a big plot in Forest Lawn Funeral Home to be with the other rich people. She didn't want to *rot next to ditch diggers*. She had pushed and bullied the rep for the best possible space at the cheapest possible price.

"Mother... Mother wanted..."

*Can you imagine your life, without me here!*

The room began to sway and Malcolm felt his legs buckle beneath him.

"It's a hell of a lot to go through," a young Hispanic police officer was saying as he helped Malcolm to the sofa. "Lost *mi madre* last year. *Devastador*. Really gets to you. Guess we're always their little boys?" He offered a knowing smile. "You'll get through this." He patted Malcolm reassuringly on the shoulder.

Malcolm lost the remainder of the afternoon to sorting papers and calling people. He notified the cemetery of his mother's last minute change of heart, of not wanting to be buried in the *cold ground*, opting instead for a *warm* cremation. *Completely understandable*, they empathized. And he'd prefer to keep the ashes at home, to keep her close. *So many do*, they assured.

Her team of doctors, nurses, care workers and therapists offered a veritable garden of flowers and condolences. Her lawyers offered assistance with the upcoming lawsuit. Malcolm learned that the failed battery was currently being recalled and he should expect a nice settlement for such a *wrongful death*.

Malcolm spent most of the following week working around the house. He packed up many boxes of his mother's clothes, books and medical supplies for donation to a local women's shelter. The thought of women in need, wearing his mother's designer label clothes made him smile.

He bought himself a new wardrobe at the charity shop. Gone were the beige, grey or tan Dockers; gone were the button-down permanent press shirts of an acceptable hue. Gone also were the tortoiseshell horn rimmed glasses. He was at last growing accustomed to the new contact lenses. And he hadn't lost one behind the toilet, when putting them in, in three days. He'd even gotten a manicure, now that he longer gnawed his nails down the bloody quick. And he took down the blinds that blocked his view of the beach; of Michael.

The bedroom.

Freshly painted, with newly hung sheer curtains, it was light and far more comfortable than it had ever been before.

He stayed at the window for hours hoping to catch a glimpse of Michael as he balanced on the top of a monster wave, or paddled easily back onto sand. He watched the beach's population slowly evaporate as the sun set over the surf, and the last riders crested into shore. He pulled the curtains closed and sighed, his head falling back against the wall. He admonished himself for actually thinking he would find Michael out there, just *waiting* for him.

Malcolm had settled in for the night when he heard a knock at the front door. 11:15 P.M. A little late for visitors, but death does strange things to people. He pulled himself from the sofa to the door, opening it wide without checking.

"I thought this might help." Michael held up two 1.5L bottles of Gallo Zinfandel.

On the one year anniversary of the storm Malcolm bought six new azalea bushes. He was growing quite fond of the brightly colored flowers and planted them all around his dearly departed mother's scattered ashes.

Red from the heat of the day's sun and feeling the strain of his muscles from the work, he relaxed into too many cans of Lagunitas Hop Stoopid beer. *Cheers to you Mom*. He dozed a little as the sun scorched and slipped into the ocean.

The fullness of his bladder woke him around midnight and he stood up, stretching and taking a long slow breath.

He looked at the bushes and smiled. He unzipped his jeans and held himself facing the flowers. He arched back slightly and let go with a thick golden stream of hot piss. *Tap twice*, Mother always instructed.

*Yes Mother.*

# Freedumb in a Snow-Globe

## Spider McQueen

Stealing cars was an occupation that I gave less of a fuck about, but when he told me he made three thousand dollars a pop for high-end sports cars, I at least had some questions.

I moved into his Park Slope apartment almost immediately after fulfilling his fantasy of fucking him in the ass with a shiny, black, strap-on dildo after too many drinks. He was forty-one, hot-blooded, resembled a skinnier Tom Hanks and had a fierce meth addiction in which I soon became a willing participant. A veteran drug addict who was always teetering on the edge of loose, he was threatened with eviction on more than one occasion due to lack of payment, while maintaining a regular two gram-a-week habit whether the rent was paid or not. We argued about nothing, animal fucked and starved our bodies afterwards with chemical bewilderment until late into the candle-lit night, when he left for his unorthodox self-employment. He usually left around three in the morning, out of the fire escape in the bedroom, right into the blizzard that swept snow onto the floor like salt, with just a sweater and a scowl, unbecoming of a Tom Hanks doppelganger. He never asked whether I wanted to tag along after that initial proposition at the beginning of this lovely story, and I never asked.

No matter. I still reaped the benefits just by being eighteen and twenty-three years his junior. I loved the hundred dollar bills he squeezed into my hand when he came home well into the afternoon. His hot breath reeked of stale vagina; his adrenaline was high from a great night of thievery, which usually left us drained from hours of wretched, drug-induced sex. We weren't a couple, at least I thought we weren't, until I found out two weeks into the live-in situation that I was pregnant. When he announced with a head full of cocaine that he wanted to marry me in Vegas after this last jump-off, I decided to save up, get an abortion and move the fuck out.

It must've been Tuesday, a week before Christmas, when I woke him up after two days of catch-up sleep and told him my intentions, to which he proceeded to beat the shit out of me until I blacked-out on the kitchen floor. I awoke in his bed with my ankles and wrists strapped to the bedpost with extension cord. My face was in shambles and tied tight with underwear to keep me silent...my asshole on fire.

The apartment was empty and dark as usual. The window was open despite the cold, and a good amount of snow had fallen through, leaving a small pile melting on the hardwood floor.

I had to kill him, or die trying. I figured the latter might be more realistic considering how tight he made the knots. I wiggled maniacally until I felt warm blood careening down into my armpits and quit.

The apartment was desperately lacking the proper furniture to call it a home; just a California King bed with oak bedposts... sturdy as fuck and unmovable, a dirty sofa bed in the living room and a battered fold-out table that wasn't always unfolded, but sat in a corner of the kitchen waiting for the next bit of crushable drugs to make it useful again. The open window next to the bed led to an empty back alley via a steel fire escape that became his door during the night. Nobody sane ever ventured into that alleyway and so no one could hear me through the sweaty undershirt he tied around my head, muffling my angry screams. After all, we were in Brooklyn and it was natural for no one to creep unbeknown into a trash-strewn alley, then stop and look up at a random open window on the fifth floor and give a shit. I would have had a better chance of winning the lottery.

I yearned for the smell of fresh-cut grass at my father's house on the West Coast, and I imagined the rose-scented air filling my nostrils; the sweet sight of the California sun setting upon the horizon in a brilliant array of fruity colors.

It was all I could do to ease my mind of the hatred that grew with each thought of kissing his cold, weathered lips. It was like kissing a dead man, which it would be very soon once I found a way out of the mess I was in. He had the saliva-retention of a Saint Bernard, and I realized I loathed his kisses without the drugs. I took a deep breath to analyze my situation with a sound mind, without the anger in my empty belly boiling up into my head, without wishing I could shove my hand up his ass and pull out his liver. When I finally managed to free myself, I was going to set the whole damn building on fire and be halfway through Texas before the investigation. I eyeballed the dirty clothes decorating the floor, getting damp from the snow, and spotted a package of tobacco lying next to his empty closet. I prayed for the Cancer Ghosts to rip out a bible page and roll me a cigarette before I stewed into one gigantic ulcer of impenetrable rage.

The sky, the color of old blood.

Not a star in sight.

Almost morning…or was it already?

I hear the raindrops hit the window pane. As that first wonderful drop caught the wind that whipped through the apartment, I imagined a fierce, black windstorm that killed him instantly wherever he was. I shook a creeping smirk of childlike anarchy from my lips. The pain in my arms diminished into needles, starting the process of a future amputation. My eyes adjusted to the darkness and a half-empty pint of vodka materialized next to my left leg, causing my mouth to water. Of course it would not quench my raging thirst, but I could imagine it would stop me from thinking about this pain and anger. It was so close, yet so far out of reach. I wondered maniacally if the rim of the vodka had been tainted with cocaine before leaving the factory. What sweet bliss! The throbbing pressure in my tailbone had settled into a bedsore, and I eagerly awaited the sound of the rain so I could get a whiff of that moist air, hoping it would accomplish anything at all...cool off my temper, or at least my burning forehead.

And with the rain, I began to cry for the first time in years.

I was going to die here... with a baby inside of me.

What the fuck happened?

Was I so stupid, so frivolous with my life, so senseless of my sur- roundings, the people I met?

Hell, this was New York for fucksake!

I had to make better decisions. Listen to my gut more... the drugs didn't help. What was this baby going to LOOK like?

Armless?

Brainless?

FUCK!

How could I choose a man with such obvious sadistic ten- dencies? I prayed he had gotten struck by an 18-wheeler, his mangled body twisted and broken in the busy street like a pack- age of hotdogs.

Thank my lucky stars that I didn't marry him... I would have had to poison his spaghetti within a year's time and hope for the best lawyer I could afford on a car thief's salary.

It was beyond the middle of the night now... very close to the sun turning the sky a light gray, yet the sound of sirens and the tempered honking of expensive automobiles only intensified. Never ceasing despite the night, blending into a collage of chaos slightly out of my reach, so that I didn't even notice the tumblers unlocking the front door until after I heard the landlord's Russian accent.

I was beside myself.

I found out he was arrested the day he left for that last assignment. Thank GOD he never paid his rent on time and double thank God for that window left open to partially flood the neighbors bedroom below us, or else the landlord would have never found me in a piss, blood and semen covered bed after what I learned was four days of being tied up. I left without my dignity, but a changed woman indeed.

I left the bottle of vodka where it was.

Merry Christmas.

# INTERVIEWS

## ALAN WRIGHT

I love interviews, especially early in the day. I get up earlier than my wife and do all the things that are marginal at best on any other given day: shower, brush my teeth and hair, and even put on underwear.

It's a real technique, the morning routine. After I towel off I always do my hair first. Gel, hairspray, blow drier, and the whole works. You can say a lot with your hairstyle. I didn't use to care; I had long hair and wore it in a ponytail for interviews. But after being a manager, I know how important that first meeting is. Your hair should be chiseled like a good strong jaw. Your hair should tell somebody that you are meticulous yet smooth, controlled but willing to take the calculated risks necessary to succeed. If your hair is all you got, it should be enough to get the job.

The nose hairs get trimmed next. I don't know why, but long nose hairs always make me think child molester.

The shaving has to be slow. It's the best time of day to think. I am distinctly a man: the smell of shaving cream, the straight razor to jaw lines and the sting of the after-shave. I know who I am if only for the duration of my shave. I know who I am. This is when my decisions are propelled by confidence, not fear.

I don't shave every day, but I'm thinking, like I do before every interview, that maybe I *should* shave every day, if only for the thinking.

No nicks. They are a sign of a shaky hand, the hand of a man that can't put something sharp to his neck with ease and assurance. I get up early for this. It takes time to do these things. It takes time to hold this blade to my skin. I've had to cancel appointments for nicks. A cut just won't do.

I hope it will be a woman. I do a lot better with women in general. After all, they smell the same things I do when I'm shaving. They can smell that combination of my skin and the products used to make it smooth. They picture me in the bathroom, a towel around my waist, the shaving cream disappearing in easy clean swipes. Maybe she only thinks it a second. That's all I need. I smile probably just as she pictures me half-naked. That's when I turn on the charm. I tell them how many people I have supervised, the projects I have directed, the skills that I possess. I lean in a little to say something funny. That's so she can smell me a little more.

After shaving, I always brush my teeth and put on deodorant. I kill myself sometimes. Here I am, looking in the mirror at a guy who could rule the world if he just put his mind to it. Today I think I will. I feel the beginning of a bona fide hot streak. I'm like the ocean, swelling and rising. Nobody can stop me. Just look at that hair.

I usually wear the same suit. It's not an Armani or anything, but I look cut in it. The shirt is French Blue. It shines. It lets people know I have good taste, stylish yet subtle. From this, they infer how I handle my business, with class and dignity, someone that can represent them to the highest power, hell, God even. My pants are charcoal gray and the shoes: jet-black. My tie is an elegant burgundy, with just the right amount of brightness to offset the French Blue shirt. I could fuck James Bond's girl in this suit. Women want me, men fear me, and everyone wants to be me. Pretty fuckin great suit.

I always have to be careful when I leave the house dressed like this. My wife goes crazy for me. Which is great, but I can't be ruffled or wrinkled, my hair is perfect and my mind is busily working out my destiny. I do not have the time for a ride.

I kiss my wife gently and whisper her name as if she is an angel I fear scaring off. I leave without eating, hunger gives me an edge, though truth be told, I'm not even really hungry. I take the station wagon and creep my way down the gravel driveway. I can hear the crunching the tires make; sometimes the sound of gravel beneath the car is unsettling. It sounds too real, like maybe it's the sound the earth makes as it spins through our solar system. It's easier to breathe when I pull onto the pavement and head towards Santa Rosa, the tires humming their familiar hum.

I usually drive in silence and meditate. I try and tune into what is important, like getting to the interview on time. I don't like to be late. Then I have to come up with an excuse, immediately putting me on the defensive. I've had to cancel appointments for this too.

When I walk in, it's all smiles, not salesmen smile, but comfortable with myself and everybody else smile. I don't spend my time talking too much to the receptionist, even though she obviously wants to. I have to appear single minded and focused. The receptionist will always be there. I sit and glance through a magazine, legs crossed, nonchalance at its best.

The receptionist tells me I'm going to be speaking with a Ms. Keller. Maybe she sees it, maybe she doesn't, but my smile widens just a little bit more. As she leads me back through the office, I look at her ass. I wonder if she wants the suit or me. I'm still staring at the ass when the hallway ends and the door to Ms. Keller begins. I smile my best smile, wink at the receptionist, and walk in to meet my destiny.


The office is pretty much a square of pool water blue. It almost stings my eyes in a pre-adolescent chlorine flashback. She has documents framed and arranged all over the walls, as well as the required impressionist landscapes and inspirational readings. We introduce and shake hands. I shake firm, whether it's a woman or man is of no consequence. A weak handshake feels slimy and insecure. A firm handshake is decisive and comes from men of vigor. It tells her I know I'm the man for her, however she needs me.

Her name is Gloria Keller. I knew a girl named Gloria when I was a kid. She rode the same bus as me. We use to sit in the back with the other eighth graders and talk about sex and smoking pot, what we were going to do when we could drive, who could get us beer. We made out a couple of times, while we rode home from school, never anything more than that. I always thought she was a pretty cool chick. She had this laugh. No prissy snicker: no schoolgirl giggle, this girl threw her head back and roared. It was a sexy laugh. It made me want to make her laugh. Her laugh made me feel good, a feeling I was beginning to forget at thirteen.

Gloria, as I've been asked to call her, motions to the chair in front of her desk as she walks behind. She has a big desk, not a fancy desk, pretty standard issue, but huge. She has some pictures of a man and a dog strategically placed around her computer and Rolodex. The blue of the room is really starting to bother my eyes. Gloria smiles and I flash one back as I take my seat. This is a good-looking woman. Blonde with damaging green eyes and a low cut black silk shirt. Her skirt is sleek and slit over high-heeled shoes. James Bond would be lucky to get this girl, especially after I walk into the room.

I sit down. I sit down into a deep, soft, and noisy leather chair. I'm expecting a firm, uncomfortable seat; instead I get this. My ass hits the seat and keeps on going. I overreact and jerk my arms forward to catch myself from falling the extra three inches into plush. Quickly, I recover and smile at Gloria, as if we share some inside joke. I adjust myself, inching back in my seat, loudly, across the leather.

Gloria leans over her folded arms, resting comfortably on the desk, and asks her first question. As I answer I can't help but notice how things have changed. When I walked into the room, I was a good six inches taller than Gloria was in her heels. But sitting in that soft cavernous chair, I have to look up at her. Everything on her desk is at eye level to me now. It seems she has to lean forward in order to see me. She has the look of a vulture.

It's impossible to sit up straight. If I lean into the concave back, I'll be literally laying back, as if I am in my living room, not an office. If I try to sit up straight in the middle of the seat, I end up bobbing along from side to side trying to maintain my balance in this sea of leather. For one crazy second, I see Gloria as a lifeguard, perched up high on her stand, blonde hair flowing, and her tanned skin just barely contained in her revealing yet ready for action bathing suit. I want to just stand, but I'm afraid I may intimidate her.

I can feel something drip down the back of my neck. I suppress the thought of some kid splashing water behind me, and instead remember my hair. My composure is perfectly balanced on the edge of this chair, and my hair is perfect.

The interview starts and ends without much fanfare. She asks all the standard stuff and I respond with all the right answers. She asks me why I left my last job. I tell her it was a difference of opinion. She smiles and asks if she can call my last job for a reference. I smile and lean close, "What are you, a lifeguard?'. Her smile falters. I tell her that feelings were hurt at my last employment. A substantial amount of money could have been made had my wishes been fulfilled. I expressed my views intensely in an impromptu exit interview on my last day. I tell her that bridges may have been burned. Her expression never changes.


She didn't walk me out and the cute little receptionist must have been on break because a security officer was sitting at the desk giving me an eye all the way out the door. The sun was high in the sky. I left my wife a message, knowing she was already at work, while waiting for my bagel and coffee at the shop across from my interview. My wife knows I have friends in The City and since I'm already in San Rafael, I might as well take the extra 20 minutes and go have some fun. We talked about it last night. She'll have a girls' night and expect me home late.

I page one of my friends and leave my code: 007. We'll meet at his place. As I ease into my wagon, I feel a sense of accomplishment begin to settle over me. The heat of my car only magnifies the sensation. I can't help but smile as I catch a glimpse of myself in the rearview mirror. It's intense how this shirt sets off my eyes. The strangeness of my interview, I just couldn't shake the pool; and Gloria's unexpected coldness and stupidity, are overshadowed by the completion of my goal. I was on time; I looked good and stayed on my game under pressure. I love it when I'm productive.

With the parking lot behind me, my feeling of accomplishment is fully realized and stable. The ride to the city is beautiful, open road meeting open sky. The fog that gently rolls in over the bay and through the hills is like dragon breath floating through teeth. I drive fast, humming across lanes and around traffic. I feel good. The city is on my mind and the world is opening up. As the Golden Gate Bridge looms large, it seems as if it was built for me. It welcomes me. This is a place for me to be Great.

The day is warming up nicely under this high sun. It's almost too warm to wear the jacket, but I decide to anyway, I don't want to mess with a good thing. I've been waiting for Nick for over an hour and he's starting to piss me off. I call him and he says he is still working even though I paged him 30 minutes ago. I tell him to quit sucking those guys' dicks and get into The City and party with me.

Somebody's chocolate is melting on the sidewalk next to my foot. I'm feeling antsy, like I'm waiting for something to happen. A blonde with her dog watches me stand, we eye each other, as she passes by I can smell her perfume. The bright sun glares in the windows of storefronts reflecting shiny new cars and beautiful women of every shape and size. Though no one seems to notice me much, I feel special. Someone will notice me. My morning's success and the sun's vibrant touch energize me with optimism. I can't help but imagine myself as someone with presence on these City streets. My demeanor commanding as I await my companion, with whom serious matters will be discussed.

Nick rides by as I converse with dignitaries. I yell, "Fag" and flip him the bird. People notice me now. I imagine the impression my smile and attitude leave on passersby.

Nick's apartment is right around the corner. He has to find a parking place, which is easier with the bike, but will still take time, so I stroll on across the street. I wonder what the driver of the Lexus thinks about me as I cross in front of her; I wonder if she thinks I'm on a lunch break or maybe a successful criminal. I want her to think something about me, I want to strike her, I want to consume her thoughts if only for a second, I want her to forget her husband, kids, job, her fucking well-being, and anything else that stops her from thinking about me. I want to have this effect on everyone. I want everyone to Believe. I am somebody.


Nick complains of a hangover as we rush up to his place to smoke a bowl before hitting the bars. He says "I threw up twice this morning before work, but still managed to be productive for the three hours I worked." He asks me how the interview went, and I tell him good, that I nailed it, that I would tell him more over drinks, and that I was dying to get high.

Nick pushes open the door to his apartment and asks me "Have you already started drinking." I tell him no. "You smell like alcohol, I thought maybe you got a few at the bar waiting for me." Then I remember the shots of vodka I did before going to sleep last night because I was feeling restless. I tell him this and that I thought vodka was supposed to be odorless. Nick said he thinks "it depends on how much you drink, a little is odorless, but if you drink a lot it doesn't matter what it is, you're going to smell.

Shit, I hope you didn't smell like that on your interview." I tell him it probably just started sweating out of me as I sat out in the hot sun waiting for his sorry ass to show up.

Nick's apartment is cool. It's an old 1930's place in the yuppie ghetto on Russian Hill. It was hip because of the high priced food, coffee shops, bookstores, and if you went about 6 blocks up there were transvestites, hookers, pimps, little gay boys dressed to flounce, and enough heroin to satisfy the most popular rock star. I like places like this, there's enough for you to identify with, feel awed by, superior to, sympathetic with, and forget about quick enough to make you want to get up and do it all again.

Nick and his roommate chat and settle things while we smoke. His roommate is paying the rent later, so they're figuring out the rest of the bills while they are at it. The weed is nice, but I'm feeling agitated about the whole vodka thing. I knew I had to be careful about how late I drank. I didn't have too many beers through the night but I just couldn't sleep. So around two, I had a few shots of vodka. I needed the rest to be sharp for this morning.

I don't have my ID, everyone under 35 gets carded in the city, so I strike a pose in the hallway and ask the roommate if he would ID someone that looks as dapper as I do. His roommate said "no way, especially if they were balding, like you."

On the walk to the bar, I keep thinking, now why the fuck did he go and say that? I wasn't asking him about my hair, I was asking him about my sharp appearance. Balding. I don't even think of it as balding, so much as, a cowlick. When my hair is combed just right, which it is right now, you can hardly even tell that there is a little extra skin. It's really just a few ornery hairs that need some extra attention. I don't think I like Nick's roommate, I don't trust him, and I'm keeping my eye on him.

• • •

The Monarch is a little pub down the street from Nick. It has a lot of red velvet, fake ferns, and high backed oak chairs. I like sitting in the chairs instead of at the bar, I feel regal with all the velvet, and my feet up on the table, as a beautiful blonde brings my gin and tonic. I'm in the middle of my interview story when she brings my drink, she's gorgeous and knows it and I casually take my drink without really acknowledging her presence. This drives beautiful women crazy. She'll go back to the bar a little upset and wondering what makes me think I'm so great as to not be wowed by her appearance. She might even stir up a little anger towards me. If I hang out long enough, that anger will turn to something else as she observes my swagger and charm. She's mine if I want her.

Talking about the interview brings back the smell of chlorine; I decide to omit the craziness about the pool. I know it was just some kind of freak anxiety, but still it nags my thoughts throughout the story. As I weave on, it seems to become more and more fictional with the only truth being that feeling of flailing in the pool. I do let them know I completely nailed the interview and expect a call back though I am not sure if I will actually take the job.

Nick asks "how many interviews you been on since you left us?" I think seventeen, but I tell him I'm not sure. His little smirk annoys me, so I ask him what's so funny. He says, "Seems like you've been going on an awful lot of them, yet none of them seems to work out, I wonder why that is?" Smirk big as GOD on his face. I tell him I'm not afraid to hold out for what's right for me. I don't need the easy external gratification of someone telling me I'm the one for them. I choose what's right for me by my own internal standards. I want to be in a place where I can grow, where I'm respected, and where I can truly make a difference. That's why I quit that lame job he's working right now.

"That's bullshit. You didn't quit that job, you got fired." His roommate laughs; I knew I didn't like him. I can't believe I have to explain again the difference of opinions that led me to leave that job. Yes, there were heated arguments, some incorrect accusations on the part of management, and some definite bad feelings, but I did not get fired. Nick and his roommate give each other a little look, and I think that the roommate may die before this night is over. Anyway, I tell them, I don't want to talk about past shit, the day is new, the sun is bright, and we are young and brimming with testosterone. What new worlds shall we conquer today?

We step into the afternoon sun, our differences left in the bar. There are no new worlds to conquer today, but plenty of familiar terrain to plunder and that's just fine with me. I love days when I go on an interview. I'm up early, dressed to kill, and productive, I've done my duty, I've looked for a job, and now I can party guilt free. I'm ready for strong drinks, loose women, and powdered drugs. I tell them this to a full round of smiles. I love it when the people are with me.

The fifth bar we stopped in is the one we scored the blow. It's also the one we haven't quite managed to leave. Nick's running the pool table, his roommate is running the bartender and I'm in the bathroom for probably the two hundredth time tonight. The fat lines on the back of the toilet go through my head with force, a bulldozer shoveling my synapses into crispy fried piles. I see myself in the mirror through the haze of a good time. Pupils pinpricked my eyes bloodshot and the sweat and smoke of the day has mixed with my gel and hairspray to create an Einstein effect on my head. I love it. Good hair is important on nights like these. It lets people know I am serious about my fun. People notice someone with hair like this. The little black haired girl with the pierced face should love it.

The cocaine cracks and pops in my ears. My thoughts race with the day and the night ahead of me. The creeping suspicion that just maybe I didn't nail that interview is taking more and more of a foothold in my brain. But, the thing is, it really doesn't matter, the night is still young, the interview is long gone, and there's plenty more blow. It's not as if I really need the job, my wife already has a good job. Some men would be intimidated, maybe even ashamed to be supported by a woman.

I think it suits me just fine.

# THE BEAUTY OF FINISHING

## TRAVIS N. HIPP

There were those that, when asked, would say that his life had been valuable; that it had been lived with passion and a never-ending quest for the answers to questions of mankind's meaning and meandering. That he had followed his heart to the end of the world and brought the best of it all back with him.

But as he stood overlooking the torrent of blue-grey ripples below, he sighed. All of those things left undone, words stored in memory banks waiting for opportunities missed to come around again, still haunted him.

Of course, one would be hard pressed to extract such a confession, for he had been taught that what a man has not done is a private affair, a burden for him alone to carry, and out of respect for himself and those around him, he must not allow these things to be known.

"Once an artist deems his masterpiece finished, he mustn't return to the canvas. He may feel free to look upon it so long as he knows that he will only see his failures exposed. Amongst the praise of onlookers, he will only see the lack of perspective, depth, composition and the wanting for the breath of life in the final product, and this, he alone must face."

His father had told him this. A well-known art critic in his own time, but only after discarding his own young talent for prose and paint. Almost word for word he had delivered the speech, over and over, until his carelessness at the wheel had abruptly silenced him.

"Untimely death" was the expression papers had used to describe the final moments of his father's life, and he had thought it to be a rather criminal contradiction. How could the moment that we have been programmed to live out, since the beginning of life, be called anything other than exact, determined, precise, or timely?

He gained this perspective only in his later years, when most of life's opportunities had passed him by; when there was little left to do but wait out that precise moment, guarding the secret pangs and desires of a man unfulfilled.

Had his father only done the opposite; had he only recounted to his son the endless trail of unforeseen changes that had snatched freewill from his hands. The changes that had left him resigned never to revisit his past, perhaps his son's life would have been given more meaning, more life within a life.

Had he, the son, not approached all of life's bridges with a cautionary eye, examining the waters flowing underneath, reviewing the quality of stone or steel used in its construction; and instead thrown himself off of them and into the waters to see where their flow would take him. Perhaps now, on the brink of timeliness, he would actually feel fulfilled.

Perhaps he would have had a child whom he could have taught the lessons of living life bravely, without fear, the beauty of finishing a thing and leaving it to the world to critique, instead of never letting it leave the close and confidential confines of the cloister.

Perhaps he would have let words spill forth onto the page without prejudice. Had he allowed enough of his conscience to bubble up and burst through the membrane dividing thought and action, he might have liked what he would have seen.

Had any of this happened...but it hadn't.

The woman with whom he had shared much of his life had sensed this lack of forthcoming, this thinly constructed veil between his reality and his relative past. She had prodded, she had pried, but his father's stonewall teachings had kept her at bay.

He had awoken this morning to a bed still warm from her body's weight, a pillow still strewn with her scent and a few stray hairs as a keepsake. Her drawers were empty, but no trace of malice was to be found, all were closed back caringly, the laundry folded and a pot of coffee sat hot upon the eye.

One simple note told him everything he needed to know, and had known for quite some time.

"I tried, I needed more. You wouldn't."

He needed no more explanation, justification or reason. He had known since her first questions, and his subsequent refusals to answer, that this day was in the making. He had thought himself prepared for it.

Nonetheless, this morning, he found himself wandering. At first, it was around the house, opening and closing empty drawers; then around the neighborhood, waving and mumbling empty salutations to the people out and about. Now he found himself here, on the edge of the bridge crossing the wide swath of eternal motion, leaning over and staring into the untested waters. He paid no attention to the moss covered stone pillars, long ago scrutinized. He ignored the rumble of traffic at his back and forgot his habit of looking for cracks in the façade. He finally ignored the voices of his past and did what he had been aching for. He let go, and fell, open armed, into the stream to see where it would take him, for the first and last time in his life.

# ABOUT THE AUTHORS

**Clodagh O'Brien** has been published in many interesting places. A Dublin resident, she prefers to write in bed and realises there are too many books in the world to read before she dies. She is the Assistant Editor of poetry and short fiction at the online literary journal, The Bohemyth. You can find her writings & musings at www.clodaghobrien.com.

**Michael Cooper** is member of PoetrIE and a MFA student at CSUSB who is fascinated by the fragmentation of language. He can be found in Shuf, BlazeVox, Camel Saloon, and many others. He feels we are at our most beautiful at our point of failure: orchids in the same vase of water.

**Brice Ezell** is writer and columnist for *PopMatters*. He also contributes to *Sea of Tranquility* and *Glide Magazine*. He will soon be pursuing his PhD in dramatic literature, and is currently finishing his first play.

**Jim Doering's** stories have been featured in *Meat For Tea Magazine*, *Mad Scientist Journal* and *Kansas City Parent Magazine*. His short story collection, *Sacred and Profane,* was released in February, 2014. He lives in Kansas City. His email is jimdoeringwriter@yahoo.com

**Jeffrey Sykes** has written poetry and songs since childhood. After working as a journalist he's begun to explore his dream of writing fiction. A student of history, he enjoys good writing in all forms. On Twitter @jeffreysykes

**Travis N. Hipp** is a freelance writer, musician, teacher and certified project manager. He has walked across Spain, plays bass guitar, and speaks Spanish. He and his wife and daughter split time between Winston-Salem, NC and Chile. Contact: travishipp@gmail.com or indieanthejones.wordpress.com

**Emily Auman** is a 21-year-old whose greatest pastimes almost exclusively involve alcohol and poorly-written television shows from the early 90s. She resides in the foothills of North Carolina and firmly believes the term "foothills" is a weird one.

**Barclay Jones** plays the corporate game by day and fights zombies by night. He lives by his own rules and encourages you to do the same. Some of his work can be seen on Old 67.

**S.T. Strelitz** is an MA student at the University of Central Florida. She has been writing — on napkins, on the back of her hand, in Moleskines, etc — since she was a pre-teen. She is intrigued by the human imagination, and this interest spurs her writing.

**Donald George Losey** was born in North Carolina in 1988. He has appeared on www.old67.com.

**Freedom Chevalier** has worked continuously in various written mediums since retiring from live performance in the late 90s, preferring to focus largely on the California Gothic and Hard-Boiled genres. Follow on twitter @ReallyFreedom and on Facebook or on her website, www.freedomchevalier.com.

**Spider McQueen** is the gun-toting ex-girlfriend you don't bring home to mama. She learned her story telling as a young vagabond after running away from home at the tender age of fifteen. She has been on the filthy roads of alcoholism and drug addiction , is a painter, a musician and an author of many abstract concoctions, Spider prefers to remain in her circle of the weird and the eccentric.

67 Press is a literary publishing collective founded to give fringe authors a vehicle to be heard. Our goal is finding talented people on the edge of society with something to say, who don't fit into a neat little box for mainstream publishers. We find talent and help that talent work within their vision to create a finished product. We do all the things that other publishers do, but we do it with the author in mind, not the bottom line or focus groups. We would never tell an author their book doesn't fit into a specific genre, it's too audacious or "we just don't think it will sell". We believe great stories and great writing transcend subject matter and audience.

If we sound like a publisher you want to work with, please contact us. We'd love to hear from you.

http://67press.com/contact-67-press/

www.ingramcontent.com/pod-product-compliance
Lightning Source LLC
Chambersburg PA
CBHW050948120626
46552CB00001B/433